Le Roy C. Cooley

Easy Experiments in Physical Science

Le Roy C. Cooley

Easy Experiments in Physical Science

ISBN/EAN: 9783337390150

Printed in Europe, USA, Canada, Australia, Japan

Cover: Foto ©Andreas Hilbeck / pixelio.de

More available books at **www.hansebooks.com**

EASY EXPERIMENTS

IN

PHYSICAL SCIENCE.

FOR

ORAL INSTRUCTION IN COMMON SCHOOLS,

BY

LE ROY C. COOLEY, Ph. D.,

PROFESSOR OF NATURAL SCIENCE IN VASSAR COLLEGE.

———————

NEW YORK ·:· CINCINNATI ·:· CHICAGO

AMERICAN BOOK COMPANY

PREFACE.

It is coming to be very generally believed by educators that one of the most important aims of primary instruction should be to discipline the child to habits of quick and accurate observation, and to the power of making simple but correct inferences from the facts which his senses reveal. Surely this result can be reached more easily by means of those facts which nature communicates through the senses than by subjects which have no natural dependence upon material forms; and hence the superior adaptation of the simple facts of physical science to the wants of common-school instruction.

But the only way to strengthen mind is to make it work. If the senses are to be developed and disciplined, the child must be allowed, and, if need be, compelled, to *use his senses* for himself. The teacher is to *guide* him, but not to *carry* him. His mind is to be directed toward material things, and taught to see their forms and characters as they themselves present them. The instructor is to be his *guide*, but Nature is herself to be his *teacher*. The intelligent teachers of common-schools are eagerly asking how can this theory be wrought into practice. Lack of time and lack of material seem to almost forbid

the attempt: lack of time, because custom and public
opinion demand so much knowledge of books in all the
branches which overcrowd the primary course; and lack
of material, because apparatus other than a blackboard
and a few maps is, in most common-schools, a thing un-
heard of. It is pleasant to anticipate a time when the
higher and theoretical parts of arithmetic and grammar
shall be reserved for the high-school course of study, and
their places in the common-school left to the more appropriate study of nature. It is pleasant to anticipate the time
when every common-school shall be provided with an appropriate set of apparatus, through which Nature may teach
her simple truths to children in her own playful and child-
like manner. The time is doubtless coming when both
these anticipations will be realized, and all the quicker
will it come if teachers will only *begin the work* by using
the very little time and means already at their disposal.
Some have already begun : they find it possible to secure
time for a short exercise each day, or at least two or three
times a-week, in which they perform simple experiments
with such objects and utensils as they find at hand, much
to the delight and profit of their schools. Letters from
several of these announce their surprise at the interest
thus aroused, not only among pupils, but among parents
also. Whole neighborhoods are in some instances awakened, and it will not be difficult in such cases to obtain
money for the purchase of better means of illustration !

Now this little book is offered as an aid to the teachers

who are, or who desire to be, engaged in this work. It is made up of experiments of the simplest kind, which, with few exceptions, can be performed with such apparatus as can be collected anywhere almost without expense. These experiments are arranged in groups, each group teaching some elementary fact or principle of science. They are selected from among those which the writer has long been using in the earliest stages of his instructions to his classes, and which are now being reproduced by young teachers who have gone out into the public-schools of the State, and from whom reports of abundant success are received. There is, therefore, good reason to believe that they are practical and instructive.

But there is another purpose which this little book is designed to serve. The best teachers of natural science are unanimously of the opinion that the very best results can be secured only by allowing the student to make experiments for himself. In the study of science in high-schools and academies, good text-books are very desirable; a full course of illustrative experiments by the teacher is indispensable; but if, added to these, there can be a course of simple experiments by the pupils themselves, the value of both will be enhanced.

Now the experiments described in the following pages are such as intelligent boys and girls can make with little or no assistance. All that the teacher need to give them is encouragement, and it is believed that he would find his own work more productive if, in addition to the text-book and his lectures, this course of simple experiments could be put into the hands of every pupil in his class. Students can not too early begin to acquire the habit and the power of verifying the statements in the science which they study.   This they can do in an elementary course of study by experiments of the simplest character made with apparatus the most inexpensive.

APPARATUS.

THE following list comprises the most important pieces of apparatus needed for the performance of the experiments described in this book. The articles named in the second column may be obtained very cheaply of apparatus dealers: those in the first can be found at home in any district. A great many other things will be used, but they are too common to need even to be named here.

Fruit-cans.	Glass tubing—$\frac{1}{2}$ lb. ass'd sizes.
Ale-glasses.	Rubber tubing—2 ft.
Bottles.	Alcohol lamp.
Corks.	Flask—glass, 1 pt.
Plates.	Test tubes—$\frac{1}{2}$ doz. 6 inch.
· File.	Convex lens.
Funnel.	Violin string.
Tuning-fork.	Glass tube—for frictional elec.
Shot.	Sealing-wax.

Besides this apparatus some chemicals are necessary. All these, except some which are too common to need mentioning, are comprised in the following list. They may also be obtained of the apparatus dealers at very trifling expense.

Alcohol.	Sulphuric acid.
Cochineal.	Hydrochloric acid.
Litmus.	Nitric acid.
Sulphur.	Ammonia.

Copper clippings.

EASY EXPERIMENTS

IN

NATURAL PHILOSOPHY.

"Always bear in mind that the simplest experiments, or those most easily imitated by the pupils, are the best."—*Nature.*

INTRODUCTION.

Divisibility. *Ex. 1.*—Take a glass jar, holding half a gallon,—a fruit-can answers the purpose well,—and fill it with water. Next take a little powdered cochineal, as much as will lie upon the end of a penknife-blade, which will not be more than half a grain by weight, and dissolve it in a thimbleful of water. Finally pour the cochineal into the clear water in the jar. *Notice* the cloud-like masses of colored water slowly making their way downward. After a little time stir the water briskly, and then *see* that every part of it is distinctly colored.

Now it is said that there are as many as 30,000 drops of water in a half-gallon, and that it must take as many as 100 little particles of the cochineal to color a single drop distinctly.

In this experiment, then, a single half-grain weight of cochineal has been divided into not less than 3,000,000 pieces.

Ex. 2.—Place a goblet on the table and fill it about one half full of water. Take a piece of loaf-sugar as large as a walnut, and by blows break it into small pieces. Put these pieces into the water and stir them about vigorously. After a little time *notice* that the sugar has entirely disappeared.

In this case the body has been divided into pieces so small that, being colorless, they can not be seen at all.

Ex. 3.—Take a small piece of marble, and by pounding it reduce it to the finest powder: the separate grains are almost invisible, and yet each one of them is a piece of the original block.

We learn from these experiments that some bodies can be separated into many parts. And when we think of others which we have not just now tried, we remember that they too can be broken or cut into pieces. Now this quality of matter, by virtue of which bodies may be separated into pieces, is called *divisibility*.

REMARKS.—Teachers will notice that the descriptions of the foregoing experiments are minute and clear enough to forbid any failure in the performance of them. But these descriptions only show the *work* which teachers must do; they do not give the *language* which they must use. While making an experiment the teacher ought, by skillful questions and appropriate remarks, to keep the attention of the children upon it, so that every part of the apparatus shall be observed and every action definitely seen. Above all things ought care to be taken that the final inference is seen to be the *natural consequence* of the facts observed in the experiments. The tendency will doubtless be for the teacher to do all the talking, while the pupils rest contented with simply repeating what they hear. This should be avoided.

The pupils should themselves be made to describe the apparatus while they look at it; to announce the results as they occur; and to interpret them as fully as possible and with as little assistance as may be practicable.

No two intelligent teachers will ever work by exactly the same method, but yet the principle just stated ought to be the foundation of every plan and determine the

detail of every attempt to teach science, *in its most elementary form,* for which these experiments are designed.

The following conversation occurred between a teacher
and his class in regard to the experiments just described.
It will serve to illustrate the method of making the pupil
use his senses to acquire knowledge.

TEACHER.—I have here three substances about which
we want to learn something to-day. One of them—this
which you· see (holding it up in view of the class)—is
cochineal; another (showing it) is a lump of loaf-sugar;
and the third (showing it also) is a piece of marble. I
want to show you some things that can be done with
these, and I would like to have you to tell me exactly
what you see and learn.

1st Experiment.—Now notice (teacher takes a half-
gallon jar and fills it with water): what have we here?

PUPILS.—A jar of water.

TEACHER.—I must tell you now that the jar holds one
half a gallon; and now think a moment, whether you
have not often seen water that looked very unlike this.
Tell me, then, what you see before you.

A FEW PUPILS.—A half-gallon of *clear* water in a jar.

TEACHER.—Yes; you *all* can see that the water is not
muddy nor colored; it is clear, and you know I told you
that the jar holds half a gallon.

Now here (dipping up a little cochineal upon his knife-
blade) is the cochineal. It was not always as you see it
now. It was found in the shape of little balls about as
large as large shot, each covered with a grayish coating;
but now what do you say of it?

PUPILS.—A reddish powder.

TEACHER.—The little balls have been broken into pieces

—indeed, crushed into this fine powder. But see what I will do with it. Just the little on my knife—there is not more than the weight of *half a grain*—remember this, I will use in this way (putting a little water into a goblet and the powder into it, and thoroughly stirring them together). Now, John, come and look at this, and tell your mates whether you can see the powder.

JOHN.—There is a little at the bottom.

TEACHER.—Just a little; but where is all the rest?

JOHN.—It looks like red water.

TEACHER.—Yes; you do not see the powder *in the water*, but the water looks red because the little particles of powder are *broken up* into such *very* little pieces that John could not see them, and these little pieces are scattered throughout every part of the water.

But now look again (pouring the "red water" into the jar): who will tell me what is going on now?

SEVERAL PUPILS.—The cochineal is going to the bottom!

OTHERS.—It is mixing with the water!

TEACHER.—When we have watched these very pretty cloud-like streams of colored water long enough, I will stir the water thoroughly in the jar (doing so after a pause). Now tell me if you see any change made in the water.

PUPILS.—It is red now, all through!

TEACHER.—But you know there was a whole *half-gallon* of water and only *half a grain* of cochineal! Now let us see,—how many *drops* of water do you suppose there are in the jar? Of course you do not know, and I will tell you that it is said that there are not less than 30,000. It is thought, too, that it would need as many, at least, as 100 little pieces of cochineal to color a single drop, perfectly in every part of it. And yet the half-grain has colored the half-gallon!

Now who will answer quickly,—If it take 100 pieces of cochineal to color one drop of water, how many pieces will it take to color 30,000 drops?

PUPILS.—One hundred times 30,000 are—(after hesitation a few answer correctly) 3,000,000.

TEACHER.—That is right. Now look again at this water: it is crimson-colored,—every drop of it. Into how many pieces does this experiment show the half-grain of cochineal to be divided?

MANY PUPILS.—Into 3,000,000 pieces!

TEACHER.—Surely it was a very little thing to be broken up into such a multitude of pieces! But now for the

2d Experiment.—Let us use this little lump of sugar. What have we here? (Placing a goblet on the table and half filling it with water).

PUPILS.—A goblet of water.

TEACHER.—Now watch the sugar (dropping it into the water and stirring it about a little time). Well, what has happened?

PUPILS.—It has fallen to pieces.

TEACHER.—I will continue stirring these pieces about in the water (doing so until the sugar is dissolved); and now can you see them? Come and look. (To those who came) Well, where is the sugar?

PUPILS.—It is in the water.

TEACHER.—But can you *see* it?

PUPILS.—No.

TEACHER.—How then do you know that it is in the water?

PUPILS.—We saw you put it in there.

TEACHER.—Very good: you saw it put there, and it has

not been taken out again. But you did see it in the water at first : why can you not see it now?

PUPILS.—Because it is broken up and all scattered through the water.

TEACHER.—That is it exactly! And now you can tell me what this experiment shows us about sugar, can you not?

PUPILS.—That sugar can be broken up into very little pieces.

TEACHER.—Yes; or you might say,—it shows us that sugar can be divided into pieces which are so small that they can not be seen.

Now let us see about the marble.

3d Experiment.—George, now I place the marble upon this brick which I have brought here on purpose; won't you come and strike it with this hammer? (He does so.) There, what have you done to the marble?

GEORGE.—I have broken it.

TEACHER.—Now take one of the pieces and strike it. (He does so.) There, what have you done to the piece?

GEORGE.—Crumbled it all to powder.

TEACHER.—But not to very fine powder; but now suppose you strike these little pieces, will they be broken again? Try it, George. (He does so.) Well?

GEORGE.—The powder is fine now.

TEACHER.—Then you must have broken the little pieces up into still smaller ones. We can hardly see them separately. And now, scholars, tell me what all this shows about marble.

PUPILS.—That marble may be divided into little pieces.

TEACHER.—Very good. We have now tried three things,—cochineal, sugar, and marble. We have found that each may be divided into very little parts. They are alike in this respect, even though so very different in most others. This quality of these bodies, which allows them to be broken or separated into parts, is called *divisibility*. Can you think of other substances which can be divided? (Several things are quickly mentioned.) All these things have the same quality as you have seen the cochineal, the sugar, and the marble, to possess. What is that quality called?

PUPILS.—Divisibility.

TEACHER.—What, then, does this word,—divisibility,—mean? I will write its meaning on the blackboard for you.

" Divisibility is that quality of bodies which allows them to be cut or broken into parts."

Perhaps no other teacher would do just exactly as this one did, in conducting this exercise, but in some respects his example is worthy of careful imitation.

1st. He evidently had a *definite plan marked out beforehand*. No teacher should attempt a single experiment until he has tried it, studied it, and formed his plan for using it.

2d. His object seemed to be to make the pupils *see* clearly what occurred, and to *infer* correctly from what they saw. Let every teacher lay every plan and work out every detail with direct reference to these two results.

3d. Hence he *called upon his pupils to tell him* what things were being used and what effects produced, *instead of describing them himself*. So should every teacher do, telling the pupils only those things which the apparatus does not clearly show.

It will be found to be an excellent plan, especially after

pupils have had some experience in these exercises, to *first*, put before them all the apparatus for an experiment ready for use and ask some one pupil to describe it fully, *then* to make the experiment deliberately and silently, *afterward* calling upon a second pupil to tell you *what you did*, and upon a third to tell you what changes or effects *he saw* produced, and upon a fourth to tell you what he thinks the experiment teaches. Repeat the experiment, if need be, to bring out any essential point which the pupils did not at first discover.

It will also be well to encourage the pupils to make experiments for themselves. Call upon individuals to help you at times. Especially if, during an exercise, one is seen to be inattentive, nothing can be better than to ask him to help you in the experiment being made. Let him do some part of it which you know he can do well, and take care that he do not fail. His success will do more than any thing else can to secure his attention in the future.

The following experiments furnish abundant material for such exercises as have just been indicated. If used *at all* in common-schools, they can not fail to awaken lively interest among the scholars, and will always leave their minds in better condition to pursue their regular studies to better advantage. If used skillfully by the methods just pointed out, their own *educational value* will not be surpassed by that of any other branch of study.

THE PROPERTIES OF MATTER.

Impenetrability. Experiment 4.—A glass jar may be partly filled with water (Fig. 1). Let a block of wood of convenient size and shape be then pushed down into the water. *Notice* that as the wood enters, the liquid rises in the jar, and that it falls again when the wood is taken out. We see that these two bodies, wood and water, can not be put into the same place at the same time.

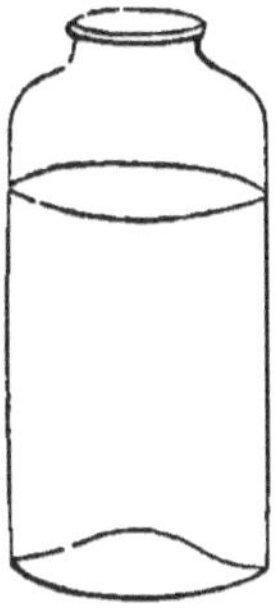

Ex. 5.—Let an inverted goblet be held with its mouth on the surface of the water in the jar. *Notice* that the goblet is full of air. Next, push the goblet down into the water. *Notice* that the goblet is still full of air, the water not rising into it. We see, here, that water and air can not be put into the same place at the same time.

Ex. 6.—Hold the inverted goblet in the water as before, its mouth being an inch or more under the surface. Having a large cork, fixed upon the end of a bent wire (Fig. 2) for a handle, push it down under the edge of the goblet and then up into the air within. *Notice* that as the cork goes up into the air some air-bubbles escape through the water. We see that air and cork can not be put into the same place at the same time.

Fig. 1.

Fig. 2.

What is seen in these experiments is true of all bodies; no two can be put into the same place at the same time. This property of matter, by which no two bodies can occupy the same space at once, is called *impenetrability*.

Indestructibility. Ex. 7.—Into a small tin cup put a little fine sugar and carefully weigh them. (See Ex. 32, Fig. 7.) Add water enough, afterward, to dissolve the sugar. *Notice* that the sugar has all disappeared. Next place the cup over a stove or a lamp-flame, and continue the heat until the water is driven away and the cup and its contents are thoroughly dry, taking care that nothing is lost by boiling or flying over. *Notice* that the sugar is to be seen in the cup again. Finally weigh the cup and its sugar; the weight should be the same as before the sugar was dissolved. We see that sugar may *disappear* without being *destroyed*.

Whenever any substance disappears from any cause, its form is changed, but the substance is never destroyed. This property of matter, by virtue of which it can not be destroyed, is called *indestructibility*.

Elasticity. Ex. 8.—Take a piece of steel wire and hold one end firmly in one hand. With the other hand take hold of the other end and pull it over to one side. *Notice* that the wire yields to the force of the hand. Next, let go the end which has been pulled away, and *notice* that it springs back to its former place. We see that this wire will yield to a force and spring back again when the force is taken away.

Ex. 9.—Having a glass ball—an "agate" used by boys in playing "marbles"—drop it upon a stone or other hard surface. *Notice* that it bounds upward to considerable height. Now the ball bounds because it is, for the moment, flattened a little just where it strikes the stone, but at the next instant it springs back to its former shape, and this *springing* back throws the ball upward. This being so, we see that even glass will yield to a force and afterward spring back.

This property of bodies, shown by the wire and the glass, by which they spring back to their former position or shape after having yielded to some force, is called *elasticity*. All bodies are more or less elastic.

Ductility. Ex. 10.—Hold the middle of a small glass tube in the flame of an alcohol lamp until about an inch of its length is made red-hot. It will be necessary to roll the tube over in the flame constantly to heat it on all sides alike. When heated to redness, take it from the flame, and *at the same time* pull with both hands lengthwise of the tube. *Notice* that the glass is drawn out into a long and thread-like wire.

Many substances, like glass, may be drawn out into wire. Metallic wires are very common. The property of matter by which a body can be drawn into wire is called *ductility*.

Ex. 11.—Taking hold of the ends of the glass still attached to the wire, use them as handles, and on moving them about, *notice* how *flexible* fine threads of glass are.

Ex. 12.—Break one handle off, leaving the fine wire still attached to the other. Put the fine end down deep into a vessel of water and the other end in the mouth. Blow strongly, and *notice* the bubbles of air coming in a steady stream up through the water, showing that the fine thread is still a glass tube. It can not be drawn so fine as not to be a tube.

Combustibility. Ex. 13.—Take as much potassic chlorate as may lie, upon a penny and mix it with an equal quantity of sugar. Put this mixture upon a piece of card-board resting on the top of a goblet. Add next two or three drops of strong sulphuric acid, and quickly take the hand away from over the mixture. *Notice* that a violent and surprising combustion immediately follows.

Wood, coal, oil, and many other bodies burn freely. This property of matter, by which it is able to burn, is called *combustibility*.

Explosibility. Ex. 14.—Let as much potassic chlorate as may lie *on the point of a penknife-blade* be put into a mortar with the same quantity of sulphur. Larger quantities can not be safely handled. Next rub the mixture with the pestle. *Notice* a sharp report or perhaps several reports in succession if the rubbing be continued.

Gunpowder will explode when touched with a burning match, and some other substances have the same property. This property of substances, by which they may be made to explode, is called *explosibility*.

ATTRACTION.

Gravitation. Ex. 15.—Let a ball be dropped from the hand. Its falling toward the earth is an example of what is seen perhaps every day of our lives. All bodies fall toward the earth.

But not only is this true; the astronomer finds also that all the heavenly bodies are pulling each other toward themselves. Indeed, all bodies tend to approach each other. The attraction which pulls them toward each other is called *gravitation*.

Cohesion. Ex. 16.—Take a half-sheet of letter-paper and gum each end to a smooth bar of wood longer than the width of the paper, so that each end will project beyond the edge. (Fig. 3.) Let the bars be exactly parallel. Now with the projecting bars as handles, two persons may try to pull the paper apart. An astonishing force will be needed to do it when the pull is steady and square. *Notice* that the parts of the paper are held together very firmly. We see that there is an attraction among its parts.

Fig. 3.

Ex. 17.—An apple being cut into two halves, let their fresh surfaces be pressed together again, and *notice* how hard it is to pull them apart again afterward. We see that there is attraction between them.

Ex. 18.—Let two oullets be flattened and then smoothed on one side of each with a knife until they will fit each other closely. Next press the two freshly-cut surfaces firmly together, and afterward let them be pulled apart again. *Notice* that it needs considerable force to pull them apart.

In all these experiments we notice an attraction between parts of one body or of two bodies of the same kind of matter. Now the attraction which holds the parts of a body or of different bodies of the same kind together is called *cohesion*.

Adhesion. Ex. 19.—Having two test-tubes, or even two small cups, put some oil into one and some mercury into the other. Into the oil plunge a rod of wood and into the mercury another. Now taking the wood from the oil, we *notice* it covered with a film of that substance. Next take the wood from the mercury, and *notice* not a drop of the liquid upon it. We learn that there is an attraction between wood and oil, while none is shown between wood and mercury.

Ex. 20.—Have two cups of water: into one of them plunge a rod of wood, into the other a piece of wax, or even a candle. On taking them out, *notice* that water clings to the wood, and wets it, but not to the wax or candle. We learn that there is an attraction between wood and water, but apparently none or very little between wax and water.

Ex. 21.—Draw a crayon along the surface of the blackboard, and *notice* its particles clinging thereto.

We learn from these experiments that there is, in some cases, an attraction between different kinds of matter which holds their particles together. This attraction, which holds particles of different kinds together, is called *adhesion*. In some cases it is called *capillary force*.

Capillary Force. Ex. 22.—Let some water be colored with ink, or, far better, with cochineal. Take a small glass tube—its diameter not more than $\frac{1}{10}$ of an inch—and put one end of it into the colored liquid. *Notice* the liquid springing up into the tube quickly and remaining there much higher than it is outside.

Ex. 23.—Stand a piece of flat glass in the water, and *notice* the liquid rising a little way up along its sides.

Now the attraction, shown in these experiments, by which a liquid is lifted in small tubes or along the sides of solid bodies, is called *capillary force*.

Ex. 24.—Wrap a common bottle in a strip of blotting-paper which is as wide as the bottle is high, and fasten its edges with wax. Next fill the bottle with water made black by ink. Finally, stand the bottle, thus prepared, on a common dinner-plate, and pour water upon the plate to come in contact with the lower edge of the paper on the bottle. *Notice* that the water will be soon seen slowly rising up the paper, and in a little time it will have climbed to the top of the bottle.

Remember, also, that oil rises in a lamp-wick in the same way; that water will wet a piece of cloth throughout in a little time, if only one corner touches the liquid; that ink spreads on blotting-paper, and other similar and familiar facts. In all these cases, as in the experiment, capillary force is causing a liquid to penetrate porous solids.

Ex. 25.—Having two strips of glass—three inches long by an inch in width is a convenient size—put a narrow piece of card-board between their ends, and then

2

cement them together with a little sealing-wax. The two plates are then *parallel* and very near together—separated only by the thickness of the card-board. Take the sealed end in the hand and bring the other end of the plates down into some colored water. *Notice* the fluid instantly leaping up to some height, where it remains between the plates.

Ex. 26.—Cement two other similar plates of glass so that they shall not be parallel—one edge of the pair being in contact, the other edges being separated perhaps an eighth of an inch. Put the lower end of this pair of plates into the colored water; it will spring up quickly as before. But *notice* that its surface is in the form of a beautiful curve (Fig. 4), and farther, that the liquid

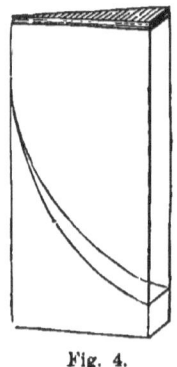

is lifted highest where the plates are nearest together.

Ex. 27.—Select two small glass tubes, one of which shall have a diameter twice as great as the other. Put one end of each into the colored water and it will rise in both. *Notice* that the fluid rises highest in the smallest tube—*just twice* as high if one tube is *exactly* one-half diameter of the other. (See *Cooley's Philosophy.*)

Fig. 4.

WATER.

Mobility. Ex. 28.—Fill three goblets, one with small marbles or large peas, another with fine shot, and a third with water. Invert a dinner-plate as a cover over each. By holding the plate tightly pressed upon the mouth of the goblet with one hand, while the goblet itself is grasped by the other, both may be turned over together without spilling the contents of the glass. Do this with each in turn, and the three goblets will be left standing, full, but bottom upward, on the plates. Next carefully lift the goblet containing the marbles, and *notice* how they spread out upon the plate, and see that they do so because they are such smooth balls, without force to hold them together. Then lift the goblet containing shot, and *notice* that they roll out upon the plate in the *same way* and for the *same reason*. Finally lift the goblet containing water, and *notice* it, also, spread itself out upon the plate just as the others did. We may give the same reason: *water consists of little,* VERY *little smooth balls, without force enough among them to hold them together.*

Because water consists of such very small and smooth bodies, it is able to move about so freely as it does. They roll over and around each other with the greatest ease. This freedom of motion among its molecules is called *mobility.* (See *Cooley's Phil.,* p. 38.)

Pressure. Ex. 29.—Having a lamp-chimney, whose lower end is smooth and even, cut a circle of tin large

enough to cover it.   Make a small hole in the center of
the disk and pass a string through it, letting a knot in the
lower end prevent the string from coming out.
Now run the string through the lamp-chimney,
and by means of it hold the tin up tightly
against the end of. the glass until it is pushed
down to the middle of a jar of water.   Then
let go the string (Fig. 5), and *notice* that the
tin—a heavy metal—does not sink.   *Notice*
also that there is nothing but water to hold it
up.   The experiment teaches that *water exerts
an upward pressure.*

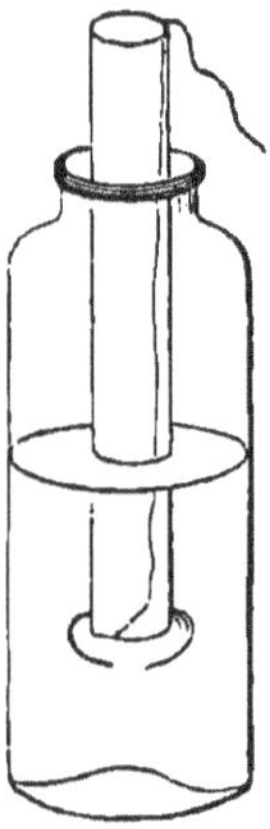

Fig. 5.

Ex. 30.—Take a glass tube, bent in two
places at right-angles,* and hold the finger
tightly over one end, or close it with a cork.   Let some
water, colored with ink or cochineal, be poured into the
other end ; it will fill that arm of the tube and a part of
the horizontal portion.   (Fig. 6.)
Now let the air slowly pass from
under the finger or the cork at
the closed end, and *notice* the
water moving *downward* in one
arm, *sideways* through the horizontal part, and *upward* in the
other arm of the tube.   By this

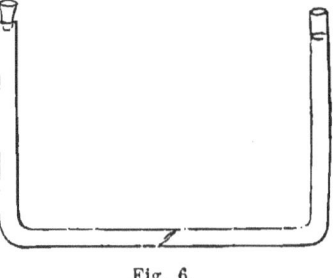

Fig. 6.

motion of the water we learn that it is exerting pressure
downward, sidewise, and upward, at the same time.

Ex. 31.—Place a small block of wood upon the surface

---

* A glass tube held in the flame of an alcohol lamp until it begins to
soften may be easily bent into any required shape.   Roll it in the flame to
heat all sides alike, and when it begins to yield, press it gently into the
desired shape.

of water in a jar, and by means of a rod of wood or iron try to push it down to the bottom. *Notice* its struggles to stay at the top, and also that there is nothing but water to push it up.

Ex. 32.—To the middle point of a bar of wood let a cord be tied so that the bar will balance when the string is held in the hand. This bar is a *very good scale-beam.* From one end hang a stone about the size of a hen's egg, and from the other end hang a small cup, into which put just sand enough to make it balance the stone. (Fig. 7.) Now let the stone be made

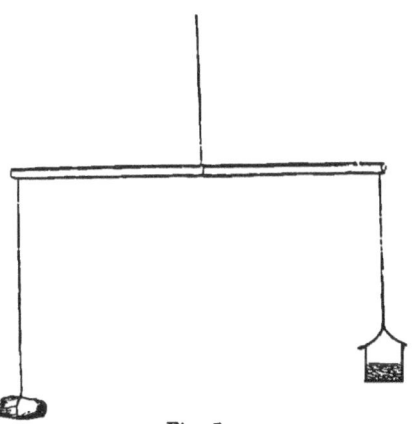

Fig. 7.

to hang down into a vessel of water. *Notice* that it is no longer balanced by the cup of sand: it is lighter in the water than out of it. See that it must be the water that helps to hold it up.

From these two experiments we learn that water presses upward against bodies immersed in it.

Ex. 33.—Fill a pitcher brimful of water. Place a dish under the lip to catch the water soon to run over, and smear the *under side* of the edge of the lip with tallow to prevent water from running down the side of the pitcher. Lay the block of wood (Ex. 31) carefully upon the surface, and *notice* that water runs over the lip. Afterward *notice* that the upward pressure of water just sustains the wood, and hence must just equal the weight of the block. Hang a cup from each end of the scale-beam; make them just balance. Now dry the wood and put it into one cup; take the water that was pushed over the

lip of the pitcher by it and put it into the other cup.
Let all this work be very *carefully* done. Then *notice*
that the wood and water just balance. We thus learn
that the water displaced by a body which floats, weighs
just as much as the body itself.

Ex. 34.—Empty the water from the cup and make the
two cups balance each other again. Then tie the stone
(Ex. 32) to one end of the "scale-beam" by a string
long enough to let it hang down below the cup, and
put sand into the other cup to balance it. Next let the
stone hang into the pitcher *full* of water and catch the
liquid displaced. *Notice* that the stone is lighter now
than before. How *much* lighter? Another experiment
will tell.

Ex. 35.—Put the water that was displaced by the stone
into the cup above it, and *notice* that the balance is restored, and *learn* that the weight which this heavy body
loses in water is just equal to the weight of water it dis-
places.

AIR.

Compressibility. Ex. 36.—Take a glass tube several inches long and pass one end of it tightly through a cork which has been selected to fit the neck of a vial. Push the cork end of this tube into some colored water and close the other end with the finger. Keeping the end closed, lift the cork from the water, and press it tightly into the neck of the vial, at the same time taking the finger from the end of the tube. *Notice* now that the colored water stands some distance up the tube —the space below being filled with air. (Fig. 8.)

Next slip the end of a piece of rubber tubing over the end of the glass tube. Apply the lips to the end of this and *gently* press the breath into it. *Notice* that the water in the tube moves toward the vial. But there is no escape for the air, and hence it must be crowded into smaller space than it occupied before. We thus learn that air is compressible.

Fig. 8.

Expansibility. Ex. 37.—Now apply the lips to the rubber tube again and draw the air out of it. *Notice* the colored water moving away from the vial, and see that the air now fills more space than before. We thus learn that air is *expansible.*

Elasticity. Ex. 38.—Using the same apparatus, let the breath be alternately pressed gently into the tube and then withdrawn, and *notice* the water alternately moving back and forth in the tube. The air first yields to the force of the breath; it then springs back when the force is withdrawn. We see that it is *elastic*.

Pressure. Ex. 39.—Place one end of a straight glass tube in colored water, and with the lips at the other end withdraw the air. The colored water is *seen* rising in the tube. It is pushed up, but *notice* that there is nothing to push it up but the air that rests upon the surface of the water in the vessel.

Ex. 40.—Push a glass jar (a fruit-can) down into a pail of water until it is filled. Take hold of the bottom of the jar and lift it until only the edge of the mouth of it is under the water in the pail. *Notice* that the jar is still full of water. Something holds the water up; there is nothing to do it but air outside

If a shelf is fastened in one side of the pail just under the surface of the water, as may be very easily done, the full jar may be left mouth downward on the shelf; the water will not run out.

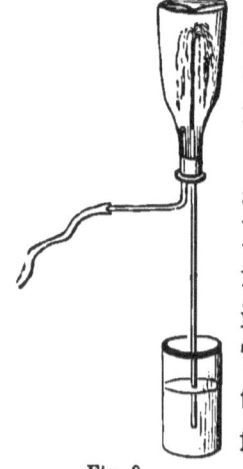

Ex. 41.—Fit a long-necked bottle with a cork through which two tubes pass. Both tubes should reach some distance into the bottle. One should reach some inches outside, the other must be shorter. To the shorter one the end of a rubber tube must be attached. Fig. 9 shows the full arrangement. Now let the lower end of the longer tube be put into colored

Fig. 9.

water, the end of the rubber tube in the lips, and let the air be drawn out of the bottle. Then *notice* a pretty little fountain springing up instantly into the bottle. There is nothing but air to push the water up.

These experiments teach us that air resting upon the surface of water, or, indeed, of any body, exerts a *downward pressure.*

Ex. 42.—Take the straight glass tube used in Ex. 39 and push it nearly its whole length under water, and then place the finger over one end to close it. Lift the tube out of the water, open end downward, and *notice* that the water does not run out of it. There is nothing but air to keep it up in the tube.

Ex. 43.—Take a *narrow*-necked bottle, and having immersed it in a vessel of water until it is filled, almost cover it with the finger, turn it mouth downward, and lift it out of the water entirely. *Notice* the water refusing to run out, and that there is nothing but air to keep it in.

Ex. 44.—Take a *wide*-mouthed bottle, or an ale-glass, and proceed as follows: having filled it with water, slip a piece of paper under its mouth and hold it against the glass until the bottle is lifted out of the water. The hand may then be taken away from the paper, when the water will be *seen* remaining up in the bottle. (Fig. 10.)

In these experiments we *see* that the air is exerting *upward pressure.*

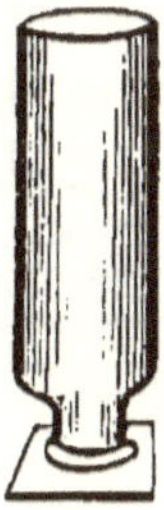

Fig. 10.

Ex. 45.—Let the wide-mouthed bottle used in the last experiment be filled with water and covered with the small piece of paper as before. Hold it in a horizontal position, *see* that the water does not run out. Turn it around to point in various directions horizontally; the water is still kept in by the air. Hold it obliquely in various directions, and witness the same result. We thus see that air exerts pressure in all these directions.

By considering all these experiments on pressure together, we are taught that *air exerts pressure in all directions.*

The Pump. Ex. 46.—Let a glass tube have one open end in colored water. With the lips applied to the other end, take the air out of the tube above the water, and *notice* that the pressure of air pushes the water up.

Ex. 47.—Next take a wire longer than the tube and wind cotton upon one end until it is so large that it can with some difficulty be drawn into the tube. Pass the wire up through the tube, and, taking hold of the upper end, pull the cotton into the other end, and then insert it in the colored water. Next pull the cotton upward in the tube, and *see* the water following it. (Fig. 11.) Notice that the air is here taken out of the tube above the water by lifting the cotton.

We thus learn that water will be pushed up in a pipe or tube whenever the air within is by any means lifted out. This is the principle of the *common pump.* (Cooley's *Philosophy,* p. 31.)

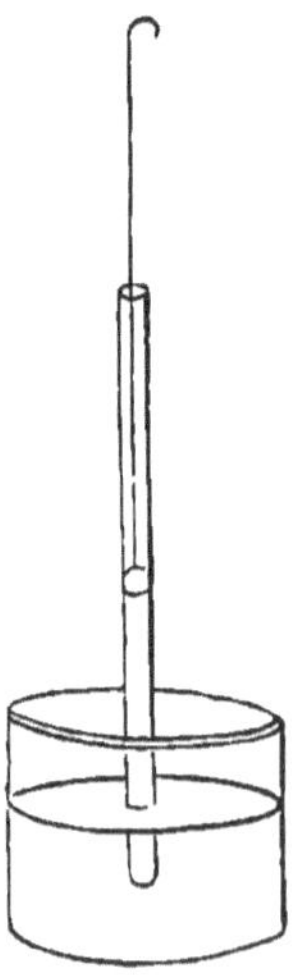

Fig. 11.

The Siphon. Ex. 48.—Repeat Ex. 42, and *notice* again that the pressure of air sustains the column of water in the tube. (Fig. 12.) Study it further. See that the weight of the water is pressing *downward;* that the air is pressing *upward*, and that the upward pressure is strongest.

Ex. 49.—Take next a glass tube, bent in the form of the letter **U**, its arms being of exactly equal length, and immerse it in water. When it is completely filled, close one end with the finger and lift the tube from the liquid. Hold it with open end downward; the water does not run out. Close the other end and open the first; the water still remains.

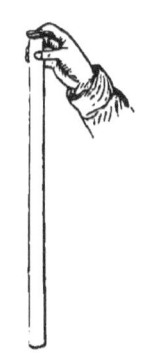

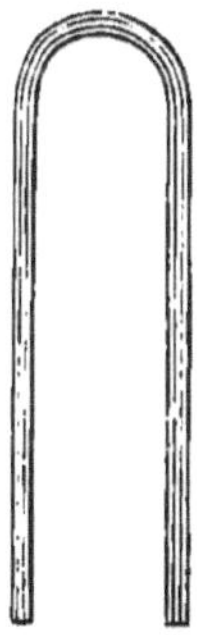

Fig. 12.

Now put the forefinger of one hand exactly under the middle of the bend so that the tube will balance, and then very carefully take the finger away from the end of the tube. *Both* ends are now open *downward* (Fig. 13), but still the water does not run out. Notice that the water in both arms is pressing *downward*—that the air at both ends is pressing *upward*. Again, see that the downward pressures, being equal, overcome *equal portions* of the air pressures, and thus leave *equal upward pressures* to keep the water from running out.

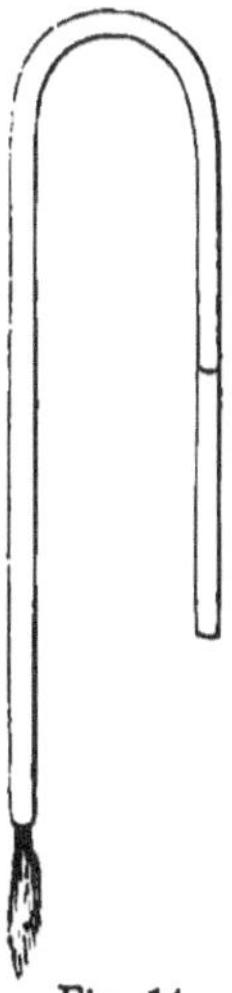

Fig. 13.

Ex. 50.—Take next a bent tube, one arm being longer than the other. Use it exactly as the tube was used in the last experiment. The water will not remain in the tube balanced upon the finger; *notice* it running out of the longer arm only! (Fig. 14.)

In this case there is greater pressure of water downward in the long arm than in the other; it *overcomes* more of the air-pressure. This *leaves* more of the air-pressure upward against the water in the short arm. This *stronger* pressure of

Fig. 14.

the air upward against the water in the short arm pushes the water *up* through it, *over* the bend and *out* of the

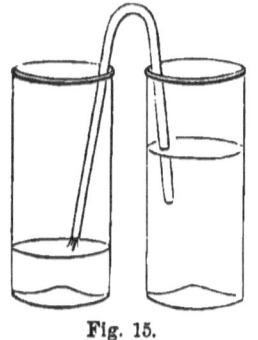

longer arm. Such a bent tube, one arm longer than the other, is called a *siphon.* It is used to transfer liquids from one vessel into another; let another experiment show how it is used, thus:

Ex. 51.—Place an empty jar (fruit-can) or other vessel, beside another

Fig. 15.   containing water. Fill the siphon with water by immersing it, and close the longer arm by holding the finger over its end, while the end of the shorter arm is being put into the vessel of water. Let the longer arm hang over into the empty vessel, and open its end. (Fig. 15.) The water will continue to run until it stands at the same height in both vessels. (See *Philosophy,* p. 73.)

The Effect of Heat. Ex. 52.—Take a bottle containing some colored water, and fit to it a cork having a hole in its center. Take the little vial and glass tube used in Ex. 36, and pass the tube through the hole in the cork of the bottle down into the colored water below. (Fig. 16.) Now apply the heat of a lamp-flame *gently* to the vial, or pour warm water over it, and *notice* bubbles of air coming out of the tube and up through the water. The vial and tube can no longer hold all the air they did.

Ex. 53.—Press a goblet bottom upward down into a vessel of water. *See* that the goblet is full of air. Pour warm water over the goblet, and *notice*

Fig. 16.

bubbles of air coming out through the water, *showing* that the air is made larger by the warmth. These experiments teach that the effect of heat upon air is to expand it.

Ex. 54.—If the bottle and vial, used in Ex. 52, have now been standing some time since the heat was applied, the air in the vial must have grown cool again. Look at the apparatus, and see the colored water standing far in the tube above the fluid in the bottle. *Notice* that the air has been cooling and growing smaller at the same time.

Ex. 55.—Pour now upon the vial some *cold* water; *see* the water mounting still higher, showing again that as the air is cooled it gets smaller.

We are thus taught that *air contracts* when heat is withdrawn from it.

Ex. 56.—Place a piece of candle about an inch long—perhaps less—upon a flat block of wood. Light it, and *notice* the flame burning *steadily*. Now put a lamp-chimney over the flame, leaving one edge of it projecting over the edge of the block (Fig. 17), and *notice* that the flame is no longer steady. Its flickering shows that air is coming under the edge of the chimney against it.

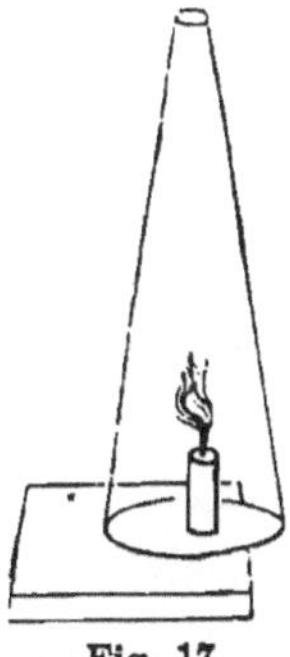

Ex. 57.—Now let some bits of light cotton or feather, hanging at the end of fine thread, be held over the top of the chimney; they will be blown away, *showing* that air is coming out of the top of the chimney.

Fig. 17.

We thus *learn* that heated air is pushed upward by the colder air beside it which flows in at the bottom to take its place.

Upon this principle the production of winds may be explained. (*Natural Philosophy*, p. 141.)

VIBRATION.

The Pendulum. Ex. 58.—Let a ball--it may be a bullet, a ball of wood, or even an apple—be fastened to the end of a cord, the other end of which is to be attached to some fixed support above. This fixed support is easily arranged by nailing a bar of wood to the window-frame, so that it will project out some distance from the wall into the room. A string may be bound around the bar, and the cord of the ball may be tied into this ring. By this means the ball is able to swing *freely* beneath its support.

A body hung so as to be able to swing freely under its support, is a *pendulum.*

Ex. 59.—Lift the ball several inches away to one side and let it go. Notice it swinging back and forth over the same path. Such a motion is called *vibration.*

Ex. 60.—Lift the ball again to several inches; let it go, and catch it with the other hand just as it reaches the point where it would turn to go back; it has swung once over its path. This one motion over its path is called *a vibration.*

Ex. 61.—Take two balls of equal length, one of lead, another of wood, or, such not being convenient, an apple and a potato may be used instead, only let them be as nearly of equal size as possible. Hang them from the

same bar, side by side, with cords of the *same length.*
Take one in each hand; pull them to the same distance,
and let them both start at the same moment. Notice
that they go over their paths and get back to the hands at
the same time, showing that:

Pendulums of different materials, other things being
equal, vibrate in the same time.

Ex. 62.—Take two balls of the *same material,* two
apples, for instance, of different sizes, with cords of equal
lengths. Release them at the same moment; notice that
they get back to the hand again at the same time, showing that:

Pendulums of different sizes, other things being equal,
vibrate in equal times.

Ex. 63.—Take two balls of the same material and of
the same size, but hang them on cords of different lengths.
Release them both at once, and *notice* the short one vibrating faster than the other.

Ex. 64.—Change the lengths of the cords, but still
have one shorter than the other, and after every change
notice that the shortest pendulum vibrates most rapidly.

We thus *learn* that the time of vibration depends upon
the length of the pendulum.

Ex. 65.—Take now two pendulums, one being just
four times the length of the other.* Count the number
of vibrations each one makes in one minute by the watch
or clock. Divide 60 by these numbers, to learn how long
each one takes to make one vibration. Then *notice* that

---

* Measure from the point of support to a point a very trifle below the
middle of the ball.

the time for the longer pendulum is just two times as great as for the shorter.

Length = 4 . . . . Time of a vibration = 2.

Ex. 66.—Let, next, one pendulum be nine times as long as the other. Count and divide as before. *Notice* that the longer pendulum takes three times as long to vibrate.

Length = 9 . . . . Time of a vibration = 3.

Now compare the lengths of pendulums and the times of one vibration, and see that:

The time of one vibration varies as the *square root* of the lengths of the pendulum.

SOUND.

Ex. 67.—Strike the prongs of a tuning-fork gently upon the edge of a table, and then stand the other end upon the table-top. The sound will be distinctly heard. Repeat the operation, and while the sound is heard, bring the edge of a knife-blade carefully alongside of one of the prongs, and notice what a rattle it causes. The prong is found to be in motion, bounding back and forth against the blade.

Ex. 68.—Let a bell be struck, and while the sound is heard, touch the bell gently with the finger, and *feel* the tremulous motion while its sound is heard.

Ex. 69.—If the bell is large, or, better still, if you have a glass bell-jar, make a little pendulum of cork, and hang it so that it touches the lower rim of the bell. When the bell is struck, *notice* that you not only *hear* the sound but at the same time *see* the tremulous motion of the ball caused by the motion of the bell.

Ex. 70.—Take a piece of violin-cord, or of piano-wire, somewhat longer than your table. Fasten one end to a nail in one end of the table, and let the other end of the cord pass over a pulley, or even a projecting piece of board, fastened to the other end of the table, and to this end of the cord hang a heavy weight—a pail or box filled with sand or stones. Let two bridges, like the bridge of a violin, be placed under the cord near the ends of the table. The arrangement is now complete.

Pull the middle of the cord to one side and let it go again. *Notice* the sound that is *heard*, and the motion that is at the same time *seen*.

In all these experiments we find that the sounds of bodies are accompanied by tremulous motions or vibrations, which leads us to *infer* that:

Sounds are produced by vibrations.

Ex. 71.—Move one of the bridges toward the other; this shortens the vibrating part of the cord. Make it sound again, and *notice* that while the cord is shorter, the sound it makes is higher. Shorten it more yet; the sound is still higher.

Ex. 72.—Move the bridge gradually back to its first position, thus lengthening the vibrating part of the cord. Make it sound after every change in length, and *notice* that while the cord is lengthening the sound is gradually getting lower.

We thus learn that the height or *pitch* of sound produced by a cord or wire depends upon its length—the *highest sound* being caused by the *shortest cord*.

Ex. 73.—Let the bridges remain stationary, and put more and more weight into the box at the end of the cord, to stretch it tighter. Notice the sound after every addition. It will be found to get higher and higher.

Ex. 74.—Next take off the weight gradually, so that the cord will be stretched less and less, and *notice* the sound after each loss of weight; it will be found to be lower and lower.

From these experiments we *infer* that:

The pitch of the sound of a cord or wire depends upon the weight or force which stretches it,—the higher sound being produced when the cord is most tightly stretched.

Ex. 75.—Take two cords of different sizes so that they may be of different weights, and stretch them over the table side by side. Place the bridges under both cords, so that their vibrating parts shall be of equal lengths, and finally hang equal weights at their ends. The lighter cord will invariably give the higher sound. From this we *infer* that:

The pitch of sounds produced by different cords depends upon their weights. Other things being equal, the lightest cord gives the highest sound.

LIGHT.

For experiments with light it is very desirable to darken the class-room and admit a small beam of sunlight with which to work. Choose a window into which the sunlight enters most directly at the time the experiments are to be made, and prepare it as follows:

Let some boards be cut of the right length, and let them be of such number and length that when fastened together by cleets they will form a shutter fitting the inside of the window and darkening it completely. At a convenient distance from the bottom of this shutter a hole two or three inches in diameter should be made, through which sunlight may come. For some experiments the *direction* of the beam of light passing through the room is a matter of importance. An addition easily made to the shutter will help the operator to control the direction and change it at will. Let a shelf be fastened to the outside of the shutter, just under the hole. Upon this shelf a piece of looking-glass may be placed. Now, by propping up the outer end of this glass, and perhaps one side of it also at the same time, it may be given just the right position to receive the sun's rays and throw them through the hole into the room. Any change of position of the glass will change the direction of the light. That the glass may be easily changed at pleasure, have a second hole in the shutter large enough to allow the hand to pass out for the purpose: this hole may be covered with black cloth when not in use.

It will not be difficult to darken the other windows in the room by closing shutters, or drawing curtains, or perhaps by hanging shawls over them.

With this cheap and easily-constructed arrangement many very beautiful experiments may be made with the greatest ease. A *looking-glass*, a small *concave mirror*, a *convex mirror*, one *convex lens* and another *concave*, and a glass *prism*, are the most important pieces of apparatus. They can be obtained from apparatus dealers at small cost.

A little time, a little money, and a little ingenuity spent in putting up and using this apparatus, will be abundantly repaid in beautiful results.

Choose a day when the sun shines brightly, and while making experiments keep the lower sash of the window raised above the hole.

Ex. 76.—Through the hole in the shutter admit the sunbeam: sprinkle dust in the path by striking two dust-brushes together in front of its entrance. *Notice* the path of the sunbeam shown by the very beautiful bar of illumined dust: it is perfectly straight.

Ex. 77.—Change the inclination of the looking-glass a little, and see the change of direction of the sunbeam in the room. But *notice* that in every position the beam of of light is straight.

We thus learn that light travels in straight lines.

Ex. 78.—Hold the convex lens in the beam of light entering the room, and see what a curious change: *Notice* that the light is brought to a point (Fig. 18) at some distance from the lens, and that beyond this point it widens out again.

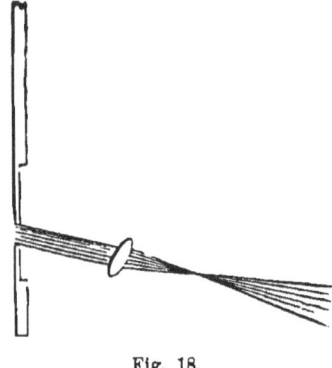

Fig. 18.

A point where light is collected is called a *focus*. The cone of light going toward the focus is called a *pencil* of light: the cone going from the focus is also a *pencil*. In the first case the pencil consists of *converging* rays; in the second the pencil consists of *diverging* rays.

Ex. 79.—Place a lighted lamp or candle on a table in the darkened room. Hold a flat piece of wood, two or three inches in width, at a convenient distance in front of the flame and catch its shadow upon a white wall or upon a piece of white cloth about as far from the wood as the wood is from the flame. *Notice* that the shadow is made up of two distinct parts—a dark center and a much lighter fringe on each side.

Ex. 80.—Form shadows of other bodies in the same way—it scarcely matters what is chosen for the purpose. The two parts of the shadow will in every case be more or less distinct.

Now the dark center is called the *umbra* and the lighter envelope is called the *penumbra*. Every shadow is made up of these two parts.

Ex. 81.—Place two flames upon the table a little distance apart, and hold the flat piece of wood in front of them, and *notice* that two shadows appear upon the wall or screen.

Ex. 82.—Then move the wood gradually toward the screen and *notice* the two shadows drawing nearer together. At length the two shadows will lie right beside each other. Carry the wood a little farther, and the two shadows begin to overlap each other, and we may *notice* then a single shadow made up of the two, its umbra and penumbra very distinct.

The umbra in the last experiment is the part of the shadow which gets no light from either of the flames; the penumbra receives light from one or the other, and is not so dark in consequence.

Just so the umbra in a common shadow is the part which gets no light from any part of the flame which casts it, while the penumbra is the part which receives light from some part of the flame, and is not so dark on that account.

Ex. 83.—The "dance of the witches" may be shown by cutting fantastic figures out of heavy card-board and hanging them by slender rubber cords from a bar of wood, by which they can be held between the flame and the screen. A dancing motion can be easily given to these figures, and the motion of their shadows will present an amusing spectacle to those sitting in front of the screen. Two or three flames a little distance apart will multiply the shadows and increase the amusement.

Ex. 84.—A circular disk of card-board, a triangular piece of wood, a cubical block, a ball, and bodies of other shapes, may be in turn held in front of a flame and their shadows formed. *Notice* the shapes of the shadows: they will change with every change in the position of the object. The disk, for example, gives a circular shadow when its side is toward the light, but only a dark line when turned edgewise. The ball, however, will give a circular shadow in all positions.

The sphere is the only form which will in all positions

give a circular shadow. The earth's shadow on the moon in an eclipse *always has a circular outline*, showing that the earth is **a** sphere.

Ex. 85.—Let a beam of sunlight into the darkened room and hold a looking-glass obliquely in its path: the light will be instantly thrown from the glass toward the ceiling or wall of the room. (Fig. 19.) If the air is well sprinkled with dust, the bars of light striking the glass and thrown from its surface will be seen distinctly.

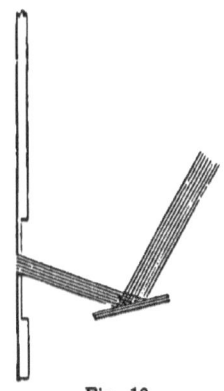

Ex. 86.—Hold a piece of bright tin or of any polished metal in place of the glass, and notice the same result.

The light which falls upon the surface

Fig. 19.

of a body is called the *incident light;* that which is thrown off is called *reflected light.*

Ex. 87.—Place a looking-glass upon the floor with its face uppermost, and upon a thick block of wood, or a book on the floor, near one end of the mirror, put a lighted candle. Standing on the other side of the glass, move around until the image of the candle is distinctly seen.

Ex. 88.—If the room is not darkened you may stand a goblet partly filled with water upon the face of the looking-glass, and then see the goblet standing upon its image—one goblet seeming to stand erect upon another bottom upward partly full of water.

Notice in these experiments that every part of the image is just as far behind the looking-glass as the corresponding part of the object is in front of it, and that the image is just as large as the object.

It is the light going from the object to the glass, and being *reflected from its surface* to our eyes, that enables us to see the image.

Ex. 89.—Take two looking-glasses of considerable size and stand them upon their edges at right angles to each other on the table, the room not being darkened. Let a vase of flowers or any other convenient object be placed between the two glasses. Three distinct images of the object will be seen.

Ex. 90.—Make the opening between the glasses much less than a right angle, and then put your face half-way between their ends and *laugh*, as few ever fail to do, at the circle of faces which is seen in the mirrors—a "surprise party," every member of which will laugh with you.

Ex. 91.—Take a bowl or basin in the dark room, and at a little distance from it put a candle-flame, so that its light may pass over the top and strike the opposite side just at the bottom. (a, Fig. 20.) The whole bottom will then be in the shade, and will look much darker than the side on which the light shines. 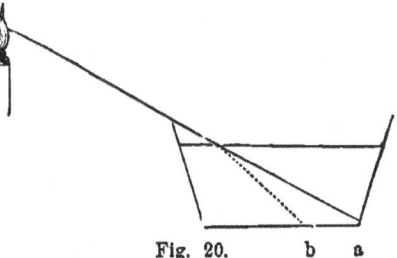 Then pour water into the bowl until it is nearly filled. *Notice* that the light now covers a part of the bottom (a b) of the vessel.

Fig. 20.   b   a

We see that in this case the light is bent out of the straight line on entering the water. Such a bending of light always occurs when light passes from one substance into another: it is called refraction.

3

Ex. 92.--The room being light, put a penny at the bottom of the empty bowl, so that as you look over the 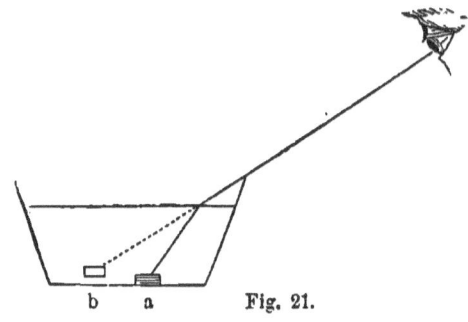 edge of the vessel it is just out of sight (at a, Fig. 21). Now pour water into the bowl carefully, so as not to disturb the penny. The penny will very soon come into view (at b), no change having occurred in the position of the vessel, penny, or eyes.

Fig. 21.

Remember that we see the penny just as we see every thing else, *by light that comes from it to our eyes.* Without the water, this light, coming up over the edge of the bowl, goes *above the eye;* for this reason we do not see the penny. But when it has to come up out of water the light is *bent* where it enters the air, and then, coming over the edge of the bowl, can enter our eyes and enable us to see the penny.

Ex. 93.—Let a convex lens—a spectacle glass can be used with success—be placed in the opening in the shutter of the dark room. The hole should be no larger than the lens: it can be made smaller, if need be, by cutting a hole of the right size in a piece of card-board, and then tacking this card over the larger hole in the shutter. Let a screen be made of thin white muslin stretched over a wooden frame. Place this screen near the lens, and move it back and forth until the best effect is found. A beautiful inverted picture in miniature of all things outside the window will be seen upon the screen. A sheet of white paper may be used instead of the muslin screen; the picture will then be best seen on the side toward the lens.

HEAT.

Production of Heat. Ex. 94.—Rub a metallic button upon a smooth board briskly; it soon will become quite hot.

Ex. 95.—Let the finger of the right hand be pressed upon the coat-sleeve of the other arm, or upon a piece of woolen cloth fastened to the desk or table, and then rubbed briskly back and forth. An inconvenient heat is soon felt.

We thus learn that heat is produced by friction.

Ex. 96.—Let a nail be laid upon some hard surface, a smooth stone, or a flat-iron, for example, and then let it be struck several blows with a hammer in quick succession. On feeling the nail. it will be found to be considerably warmed. Indeed, it can, in this way, be made too hot to be handled conveniently.

We thus learn that heat is produced by blows.

Ex. 97.—Upon some large fragments of quick-lime lying on a plate, pour some water. After a few minutes, notice the lime swelling and crumbling to powder, while large volumes of steam are escaping. Let the hand be held in this steam only for an instant, or be laid upon the plate when the action has ceased, and great heat will be discovered.

The action of the lime and water is called a *chemical* action, because the nature of these bodies is changed.

Ex. 98.—Into a cup put a small quantity of cold water, and then add about one-fourth as much oil of vitriol. The mixture will become intensely hot. There is a chemical action between the two fluids.

From these experiments we learn that heat is produced by chemical action. The heat of all our lamp-flames and furnaces is produced by chemical action.

Conduction of Heat. Ex. 99.—Take an iron wire and press a bit of wax against one side of it at a distance

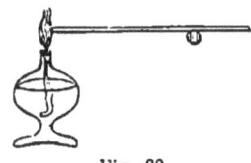

Fig. 22.

of a few inches from one end. Place this end in the flame of a lamp. (Fig. 22.) After a few minutes the little bit of wax, all this time clinging to the wire, will fall off. Now, the heat must have travelled from the flame gradually along the wire until it reached the wax, and then, by melting it, caused its fall.

Ex. 100.—Hold one end of a brass rod, a few inches long, in the lamp-flame. After a little waiting the rod in the fingers at the other end feels warm. In this case the heat has evidently travelled gradually from the flame through the rod to the fingers.

When heat travels from particle to particle gradually, as in these experiments, it is said to be *conducted*. The body in which it travels is called a *conductor*.

Ex. 101.—Take the stem of a tobacco-pipe and a rod of iron as nearly of the same size as possible, and place their ends together, lapping them about an inch, and binding them firmly with small wire. Next fasten a ball of wax to the under side of each of the rods, equally distant from the middle point of their junction. Now, if this arrangement is held with the junction in a lamp flame (Fig. 23), it will not be long before the ball of wax is melted from the iron, but it will take a long time indeed to melt the ball from the pipe-stem. We learn thus that the iron conducts heat better than the pipe-stem.

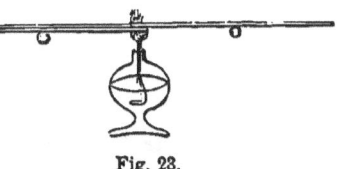

Fig. 23.

Ex. 102.—Take two wires of different metals, brass and copper, for example, of the same size and length. Hold one wire in each hand, the other end of the wire being in the lamp-flame. The heat will be found to reach the fingers through one of the wires quicker than through the other. The two metals teach us that they do not conduct heat alike.

Ex. 103.—Let two spoons, one of German silver, the other of silver, be put into the same cup of hot water, with their handles projecting. Feel of the upper ends from time to time, and notice that the silver spoon is heated quickest.

From these experiments we learn that all bodies do not conduct heat alike.

Convection of Heat.—Ex. 104.—Fill a glass flask two-thirds full of water, and place it upright in a shallow basin of sand standing on a hot stove. Very soon one who looks closely at the water will see delicate currents moving upward from the bottom. Drop a bit of blue litmus into the water. It falls to the bottom and slowly dissolves. Blue clouds appear, which, wafted upward by the currents of water, enable us to see their motion distinctly. These upward currents are of warm water, and the heat is being distributed throughout the water in the flask by their motion.

When heat travels by means of currents in the body receiving it, the process is called *convection*.

Radiation of Heat.—Ex. 105.—Heat an iron ball or a piece of stone in the stove until nearly or quite red-hot. Let it be brought out into the room by means of a pair of tongs. Hold the hand at a little distance above it, on one side of it and on another, and below it. Notice that *instantly*, no matter in what direction, the heat of the ball is felt. The air is a very poor conductor, but we find heat going through it in all directions more swiftly than it can go through the very best conductor.

Heat that is thrown through poor conductors in all directions is said to be *radiated*, and the process of distributing heat in this way is called *radiation*.

Expansion by Heat. Ex. 106.—Take a bottle having a ground stopper. When the stopper is out, warm the neck of the bottle *gently* by wrapping a cloth wet with warm water around it, and afterward put the stopper in—not too tightly—just so that it fits the neck nicely. Let the neck cool again, and when cold try the stopper. *Notice* that it is tightly held—perhaps it will not come out at all, because the neck of the bottle is so small as to grasp it too closely. Now wrap the neck again in the warm cloth, and after a little try the stopper; *notice* that it comes out easily. The heat seems to have made the neck larger, so as to let the stopper out.

Ex. 107.—Let a hole be bored through a piece of hard wood, just large enough to allow a bullet or other metallic ball to pass through, closely touching its sides. An iron rod may be used instead of a ball often more conveniently. Heat the ball or rod, and before it gets hot enough to burn the wood, try to pass it through the hole. If it has been warmed enough you will *notice* that the hole is no longer large enough to let the body pass.

These experiments teach us that heat expands or enlarges *solid* bodies.

Ex. 108.—Fill a bottle with cold water. Pass a piece of glass tube, a few inches long, through a cork fitting the neck of the bottle nicely, and press the cork into the neck. If the bottle was brimfull of water, as it ought to be, the water will stand some distance up in the tube when the cork is inserted (Fig. 24). Tie a string around the tube to mark the height of the water in it. Now plunge the bottle into a vessel of warm water. Notice the water quickly beginning to rise up the tube, and continuing to do so while the heat is applied.

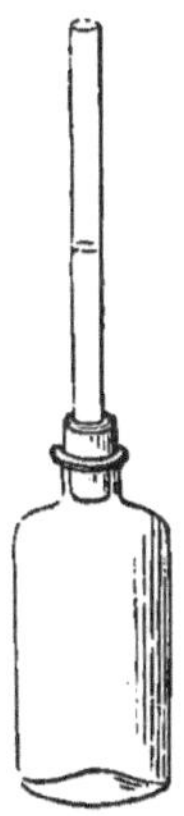

We see that the water is getting *larger* as it becomes *hotter*.

Fig. 24.

Ex. 109.—Another bottle, used in the same way, with some other liquid, as oil or alcohol, will show the same effect; the liquid will get larger as it gets warmer.

From these experiments we learn that heat expands *liquid* bodies.

Ex. 110.—Fit the neck of a bottle with a cork, and through this cork put the end of a glass tube several inches long. Into another bottle put some water, which may be colored with ink, or cochineal, or litmus. Turn the first bottle bottom upward, and put the open end of its tube down into the colored water of the second.

Notice, before going farther, that the upper bottle and its tube are full of air. Next pour *warm* water upon the upper bottle, and notice numerous bubbles of air escaping through the fluid from the lower end of the tube. The air is expanded by the heat.

Ex. 111.—After a little time, the colored water will rise some distance up the tube in the arrangement used in the last experiment. When this is the case, notice that the tube, above the water, and the bottle are full of air. Now pour some warm water again over the bottle, and see the water quickly driven down by the expanding air.

We thus learn that heat expands *air*, and when similar experiments have been made with other gases, the general truth is found that heat expands *gaseous* bodies.

Contraction by Cooling. Ex. 112.—The hot rod of iron (Ex. 107) was too large to go through the hole in the hard wood, but now that it is cold again, try it, and notice that it goes through easily again. It has given off its heat and at the same time grown smaller.

Ex. 113.—Take the bottle and tube with water, used in Ex. 108; mark the height of the water in the tube, and then place the bottle in a vessel of *cold* water. Notice the water falling in the tube, showing that as the water in the bottle cools it grows smaller.

If this does not show distinctly the desired result, then first *warm* the bottle of water, and afterward put it into the vessel of cold water.

Ex. 114.—Take the apparatus used in Ex. 52, the colored water now standing some distance up in the tube, the space in the tube above the water and in the bottle being filled with air. Pour *cold* water upon the upper bottle, and *notice* the colored water quickly rising higher

in the tube. The air is cooled by the water, and we see
that it at the same time gets smaller.

From these experiments we learn that the withdrawal
of heat from bodies causes them to contract. We thus
find that the hotter a body is the larger it is, and the con-
trary—the colder it is, the smaller.

Curious effects in Water. Ex. 115.—Into a common bowl or basin put a considerable quantity of snow, or
ice shaved fine with a large knife, and add about half as
much common salt. Stir the mixture thoroughly; it will
become nearly fluid and be intensely cold. It is called
a *freezing* mixture. Fill a thimble with water, or a pipe-
bowl, with the hole in its bottom closed with wax, and
stand this little dish in the freezing mixture. The water,
after a few minutes, will be frozen.

Ex. 116.—Now take the bottle and water (Ex. 108),
the fluid standing some distance up the tube, and place it
in the freezing-mixture.

Notice first, that the fluid sinks in the tube, showing
that as the water cools it contracts.

Notice next, after a little time the fluid stops sinking,
showing that as water goes on cooling more yet the contraction stops.

Notice again, that the water begins to rise in the
tube again, showing that the cooling water is now expanding.

Notice finally, that ice begins to form in the bottle, and
that while the water is freezing, the water in the tube
continues to rise, showing that water expands while
freezing.

Ex. 117.—Take now the bottle containing ice from

the freezing-mixture, and put it into a vessel of water slightly warm.

Notice the water sinking in the tube while the ice is melting, showing that heat contracts the ice while it melts it.

Notice afterward, that the water continues to sink in the tube for a little time, showing that heat applied to ice-cold water contracts it.

Notice finally, that the water in the tube begins to rise again, showing that after water has reached a certain degree of temperature, heat expands it. (See *Natural Philosophy*, p. 240.)

ELECTRICITY.

THE successful performance of experiments in electricity demands a *dry* atmosphere and *dry* material: dampness in either may cause annoyance and even complete failure. The winter season is generally more favorable than the summer, and an unventilated room, in which the air is loaded with moisture from the lungs of many individuals, is to be especially avoided. In a long, cold winter evening, when the family are gathered around the cheerful sitting-room fire, electrical experiments are most likely to succeed admirably. And in a school-room, which has been thrown open and well-ventilated during recess, and in which a brisk fire is rapidly heating the atmosphere again, or, better still, in the morning before the pupils have had time to load the air with dampness, electrical experiments may be tried with the best assurance of success.

The following experiments are simple enough for a child to perform, and will furnish children not only, but older students as well, with much amusement and instruction.

Electricity produced by Friction. Ex. 118.—
Take a piece of thin and tough brown paper, about an inch wide and six inches long; heat it thoroughly by holding it over a hot stove or the flame of a lamp, and then holding it in one hand by the end, quickly pull it between

the thumb and fingers of the other hand, thus rubbing it vigorously. After two or three such rubbings bring the paper near to the wall, and it will instantly fly into contact with it, and perhaps if you let go of it you will see it clinging to the wall. It will thus remain sometimes for several minutes as if pasted.

Ex. 119.—Rub the paper a second time, and, holding it by one end in one hand, bring the other hand alongside of it Notice how quickly the paper flies against the fingers, and how strongly it is inclined to stay there.

Ex. 120.—Procure a glass tube several inches in length,—a lamp-chimney, if one can be found of convenient shape to rub easily; procure also a piece of flannel cloth. Both should be thoroughly dry. Holding the glass in one hand, bring it up very near to the face; you will be able to notice *no effect*. Next rub the glass vigorously with the flannel held in the other hand, and bring it afterward near to the face as before. A sensation will now be felt like what would be caused by drawing spiders' webs over the face.

Ex. 121.—Rub the glass again vigorously, and afterward bring it near to the knuckle of your hand; a crackling sound will be heard, and *in the dark* little sparks of light are often seen.

Ex. 122.—Place some very small and light bits of cotton upon the table. Thoroughly rub the glass again, and bring it near to the bits of cotton; notice how quickly they leap up to meet it.

Ex. 123.—Let a bit of cotton or downy feather be floating in the air; bring the glass, which has been vigorously rubbed, near to it. The cotton or the feather will instantly dart against the glass through considerable distance.

Ex. 124.—Any one of the preceding experiments may be made with a stick of *sealing-wax* in place of the glass tube. The same effect will be produced.

In these experiments we see that by rubbing the paper, the glass, or the sealing-wax, a new power seems to be developed in them. All the effects noticed are due to *electricity*, and this electricity is in such cases produced by rubbing, or, as it is called, by *friction*.

Attraction and Repulsion. Ex. 125.—Untwist a

silk thread, and take one of its fine fibres; tie to the end of this a very small and light piece of cotton. Let another person hold the cotton by taking hold the other end of the thread, while you rub the glass tube vigorously. Then bring the tube near to the bit of cotton. You will see the cotton fly quickly toward the glass, sometimes through a distance of several inches. The cotton is *attracted* by the glass.

Ex. 126.—Rub the glass thoroughly again, and again bring it near the cotton; the cotton will doubtless be attracted as it was before. If so, let it cling to the glass for some time; then rub the tube again and present it to the cotton as before. If the cotton is again attracted, let it stay in contact with the glass for a time, and then go over the same work again. After a few,—sometimes only one of these trials, the cotton will refuse to again come in contact with the glass. As often as the tube is moved toward it, the cotton darts away. Not until it has first touched some other body can the cotton be made to touch the glass.

In this experiment we find the cotton driven away from the glass tube; it is said to be *repelled*.

Ex. 127.—Sometimes the electricity may be made so

strong on the glass that placing it on one side of the suspended cotton and the hand or piece of iron on the other side of it, the little pendulum will fly quickly back and forth between them many times, being first *attracted* and then *repelled* by the electrified glass.

We learn from these experiments that electricity shows its presence in two ways, viz.: by *attraction* and *repulsion*.

Ex. 128.—Let a long silk ribbon, warm and dry, be hung over the forefinger of the left hand; the two parts will hang down side by side together. Now put the forefinger of the other hand between the two parts of the ribbon and press them tightly against it with the thumb and other fingers. Pull the ribbon out quickly, rubbing the whole length of its parts between the fingers; repeat this operation three or four times, and then *notice* that the two parts of the ribbon will no longer be willing to touch each other. They *repel* each other. Put the hand between them, and both quickly fly toward it; remove the hand, and they as quickly fly back again.

Ex. 129.—Let one person rub the ribbon, as in the last experiment, while another rubs the stick of sealing-wax with the *dry flannel*. When both are well electrified, let the sealing-wax be brought between the parts of the ribbon. They will fly still farther apart. The electrified *sealing-wax repels* the electrified *ribbon*.

Ex. 130.—Now rub a glass tube, a lamp-chimney, if of convenient shape, and bring it between the electrified branches of the ribbon. Both parts instantly fly *toward* the glass: the electrified *glass attracts* the electrified *ribbon*.

We see that the ribbon acts differently toward the

electrified glass and toward the electrified sealing-wax. It flies *toward* the first, and *from* the second.

Ex. 131.—Hang a little ball of cotton to the end of a silk fibre, as in Ex. 125. Rub the glass, and then bring it in contact with the ball until the latter flies away, being repelled by the electrified glass. Rub the sealing-wax with flannel, and bring it toward the ball; the ball will quickly fly to meet it, being attracted by it. Again, we see that electrified glass and electrified sealing-wax act in different ways; when the cotton is *repelled* by glass it is *attracted* by sealing-wax.

Now whenever the electricity is like that produced by rubbing glass it is called *positive* electricity, and when it is like that produced by rubbing sealing-wax with flannel it is called *negative* electricity.

The Electroscope. Ex. 132.—Rub the glass tube or stick of sealing-wax vigorously, and observe whether any visible change whatever is produced. None: then, without some *farther trial*, it is not possible to tell whether electricity has been developed or not.

It may be brought near to the face or hand, and the feeling of cobwebs, or a snapping sound, may show that the tube or wax is electrified, or bringing it near to light bodies, as cotton, on the table, electricity will show its presence by attracting them. But neither of these ways is always quite convenient.

Ex. 133.—Now take a slender rod of some dry wood, several inches long; make a little ball of the dried pith of corn-stalk or elder, of cork, or even of cotton; fasten it to one end of a silk fibre, and tie the other end of the fibre to the other end of the wooden rod. Next place the rod upon the table, so that the end carrying the ball shall project some inches beyond the edge, or, what is better yet, put the wood up on a pile of books, or some other support, above the table, so that the little ball may swing clear.

Now notice that whenever the electrified glass tube or sealing-wax is brought near to this little pendulum, the electricity is at once shown by the motions of the ball, which, if the electricity is well developed, will fly toward the tube or wax, and, after a moment's hesitation, will as quickly fly away again.

Ex. 134.—Or, take tinfoil,*—a piece one-half inch long and one-quarter inch wide, and hang it in place of the ball in the preceding experiment, and it will be found to show the presence of electricity as well as the other.

Here then notice these simple and convenient arrangements by which to *show the presence of electricity*. Any such instrument is called an *electroscope*.

Ex. 135.—Rub the glass tube vigorously, and then bring it in contact with the ball of the electroscope; this ball, remaining in contact only a moment, if the tube is well electrified, flies away again. We have seen this action in former experiments, but what we wish to notice now is that the ball *in contact* with the glass takes electricity from it, so that it is electrified in the *same way* as the glass, or in other words, *positively*, and that when this is the case, the two bodies separate, showing that they *repel* each other.

In this experiment we see that two bodies, electrified with *positive* electricity, *repel* each other.

Ex. 136.—Next rub the sealing-wax vigorously with *flannel*, and hold it in contact with the ball of the elec-

---

* The thin metallic wrapping found on some kinds of packages at the grocery store.

troscope until it flies away, as it will do after one or more trials. Now what we must notice here is that the electricity of the sealing-wax is *negative*, and that the little ball must have the same kind of negative electricity also in it when it flies away from the wax.

In this experiment we see that both bodies, electrified with *negative* electricity, *repel* each other.

We see from these two experiments that when bodies are electrified in the same way, they repel each other. Call this the 1st *Law*.

Ex. 137.—Rub the glass tube again, and electrify the ball of the electroscope with it. Notice that the little ball is *positive*, because electrified from glass. Then rub the sealing-wax with flannel, and bring it near to the little ball. The ball darts instantly against the wax. The wax is *negative*, the ball is *positive*, and the two *attract* each other.

Here we see that two bodies, electrified with opposite kinds of electricity, attract each other. Call this the 2d *Law*.

Ex. 138.—Repeat the experiment with the silk ribbon (Ex. 128). Notice its two branches repelling each other. Now, are these branches electrified with *the same* or with *opposite* kinds of electricity? (1st Law.)

Ex. 139.—Can we find out *which kind* of electricity we have in the silk?

Rub the glass tube, and hold it in contact with the ball of the electroscope until it flies away. We know that the ball is *positive*. Bring the silk ribbon, whose branches are repelling each other. near to the positive ball, and see how quickly the two fly together! The positive ball is

attracted, and hence (2d Law), the *silk must be negative.*

We see then that our little "electroscope" not only
helps us to detect the *presence* of electricity; it also
helps us to tell *which kind* a body is electrified with.
Let us try it.

Ex. 140.—Take a piece of thin but strong brown
paper; cut from it a strip an inch wide and sixteen or
twenty inches long; thoroughly dry and warm it, and
then use it just as the silk ribbon was used (Ex. 128).
After the branches of the paper have been drawn through
the fingers once or twice, they repel each other strongly.
Now what kind of electricity have they? Electrify the
ball of the electroscope from the sealing-wax rubbed with
flannel; the ball is then *negative.* Bring near the ball
the paper, and see how strongly they *repel* each other,
showing (1st Law) that they are in the *same condition ;*
the paper is *negative.*

Ex. 141.—Electrify the ball of the electroscope from
glass : it is positive. Now rub the sealing-wax with *flannel*, and notice that it *attracts* the ball, showing the wax
to be *negative.*

Pass the hand over the surface of the sealing-wax to
remove the electricity from it, and then rub it vigorously
with a piece of *silk*. Electrify the ball of the electroscope from the glass again ; it is *positive.* Bring the
electrified wax near to it, and then notice that it now
repels the ball, showing the wax to be *positive.* It appears that the electricity of sealing-wax, when rubbed
with flannel, is *positive*, but, when rubbed with silk, is
negative !

Ex. 142.—See whether the electricity of glass is different when the rubber is flannel from that when the rubber

is silk. To do this electrify the little ball from the sealing-wax, rubbed with *flannel*, and bring the electrified glass near to it.

Ex. 143.—Take two pieces of brown paper, each about ten inches long by five inches wide; make them quite hot by holding them over a heated stove or the flame of a lamp. Place them on the table, or, still better, on a tea-tray, one above the other, and rub them vigorously with the palm of the hand. If now you take hold of one corner and lift them from the table, you will find them clinging to each other. If you try to separate them you will see how strongly they attract each other, and sometimes you may hear also a crackling sound on pulling them apart.

Notice that the *upper one only was rubbed* but that *both* are electrified. And more, since they attract each other they are electrified in *different ways*.

Ex. 144.—Take two fresh sheets of paper, such as described in Ex. 143, and, having heated them thoroughly, put one above the other on a pane of *glass*. Rub the upper sheet vigorously with the hand. Taking hold of one end, lift them from the glass, and notice that they now *repel* each other.

If Experiments 143 and 144 are repeated, it will be found that the papers whenever rubbed while lying upon the tea-tray will *attract*, but if rubbed while lying upon the glass they *repel* each other.

Now the upper one only is electrified *by the rubbing;* the lower one is electrified from the upper one. When they lie upon glass the lower one becomes electrified in the *same* way as the upper one, and hence they repel (1st Law), but when they lie upon the tea-tray the lower one

becomes electrified in the *opposite* way, and hence they
attract (2d Law).

When one electrified body electrifies another body near
to it, and puts it into a condition opposite to its own, it is
said to act by *induction*.   The upper strip of paper, when
they were rubbed on the tea-tray, electrified the lower
one by *induction*.

The full explanation of induction, or, as it is now generally called, *polarization*, may be left for a higher course
of study.

Ex. 145.—Having electrified the two sheets of paper,
show that they are in opposite conditions by testing them
with the electroscope.

EASY EXPERIMENTS

IN

CHEMISTRY.

CHEMISTRY.

The following simple experiments in Chemistry are pretty and instructive, but, as a general thing, the materials needed are not so conveniently obtained as those needed for the experiments in Natural Philosophy. They are not expensive, however, and what cannot be found at the village stores can be sent from dealers in larger towns on application.

Chemical Action. Ex. 146.—Put some strong vinegar into a goblet—enough to fill it about one-quarter full. Take some common "baking soda," as much as will lie upon the end of a case-knife blade, and sprinkle it into the vinegar. A violent foaming will occur, continuing for a time, and when it stops the "soda" will have disappeared. Add more "soda," little by little, until the fluid refuses to foam; the "soda" last added will then remain in the bottom. Now *notice:* the soda has disappeared from view in this action, while the vinegar (touch it with the tongue) is so changed as to be no longer sour.

Here then we find a violent action going on between the vinegar and the soda, by which the *natures of both these substances are changed.*

Ex. 147.—Into a common bottle put a few small pieces of copper, and then pour in upon them nitric acid enough to cover them. *Notice* that a violent action quickly begins. The fluid appears to boil. Its color be-

comes deep blue. Cherry-red vapors fill the bottle above
the fluid, and perhaps run over the top of it into the
room. The copper is, in the mean time, being slowly
used up: it will finally disappear altogether if there is
acid enough used for the purpose; and when the action
ceases, there will remain the quiet blue liquid in the
bottle, with some of the red vapors remaining in the air
above.

In this experiment we again find a violent action, by
which the nature of the substances used is changed.

Ex. 148.—Into one goblet put three or four drops of
hydrochloric acid: into another put as much ammonia.
Now turn one of these goblets right bottom side up
over the mouth of the other. Both will be quickly filled
with white fumes. The acid and the ammonia are liquids
nearly or quite colorless: they form, when put together, a
vapor which is white.

Here also we notice an action which changes the nature
of substances.

Ex. 149.—Mix together a half-teaspoonfull each of
sugar and potassic chlorate, both powdered, and put the
mixture upon a common card. The card may well be
laid upon the top of a goblet for support to keep it off the
table. Now put *two* or *three drops* of sulphuric acid
upon the mixture. A curious combustion will quickly
follow, in which tongues of purple flame will shoot up
some distance with considerable noise.

When the burning is over, look for the sugar and the
chlorate: both have disappeared, and nothing but a black
coal-like mass remains upon the card instead.

We *notice* that this combustion is an action by which
the natures of the burning bodies are changed.

Now, all such actions as have been shown in these experiments are called *Chemical Actions.* We therefore mean by the term chemical action any action among bodies of matter by which their natures are changed.

Combination and Decomposition. Ex. 150.—

Into a small vial—a long and narrow one is best for the purpose—put some water, and then add oil enough to cover the water well. Being the lighter liquid, the oil of course floats upon the water. Now pour in a little ammonia and shake the mixture thoroughly. A soapy liquid will appear instead of the oil and water. Indeed, the oil and the ammonia have joined themselves together and made a kind of soap which mixes with the water. *Notice* that this new substance, the soap, is a very different thing from either the ammonia or the oil which make it.

Now, when two or more substances disappear to form a new one different from themselves, they are said to *combine.* The new substance made is called a *compound.* The ammonia and the oil have combined to form the soap, which is a compound.

Ex. 151.—Add to the soapy liquid just made in Ex. 150, a little strong sulphuric acid. Shake them well together. The soapy liquid will in part or wholly disappear, while the oil will be brought back again and will be seen floating upon the water as before. Now we see that the sulphuric acid must have taken the ammonia away from the oil, for the soapy substance is broken up, the oil in it coming back again.

When a substance is separated into the different materials which compose it, as the soap has been in this experiment, it is said to be *decomposed.* The substances into which it is separated are called its *constituents.* The

soap was decomposed ; oil is one of its constituents, ammonia is another.

Acids. Ex. 152.—Crush one or two small pieces of
blue-litmus and put the powder into a goblet of water.
The litmus will dissolve and give a deep blue color to the
water. Now add a little strong vinegar, and notice the
curious change in color : the blue turns to red.

Ex. 153.—Into another goblet of water, colored blue
with litmus, put a few drops of sulphuric acid : the blue
is quickly changed to red.

Ex. 154.—Into another solution of blue litmus put a
few drops of nitric acid, and notice how quickly the red
color appears.

Ex. 155.—Take another goblet of litmus, and add
hydrochloric acid : the blue instantly gives place to red.

We find that there is a class of substances which are
able to turn the color of blue litmus to red. Should you
taste these substances you would find them all to be sour.
They have other characters in common, but the one most
conveniently tested is their power to turn the blue color
of litmus to red. These substances are called *acids*.

Alkalies. Ex. 156.—Take a goblet containing litmus,
the color of which has been changed to red by an acid,
and put into it a little ammonia. Notice that the red
color changes back again to blue.

Ex. 157.—Take a common glass or tin funnel, stop its
neck by crowding some unsized paper (blotting paper)
into it, and then pack the funnel nearly full of *wood-ashes*.
Pour some warm water upon the ashes, and as it runs
through them and out of the stem of the funnel catch it
in a bottle, through whose neck the funnel-stem passes

and upon which it rests (Fig. 25.) When enough of this liquid has been caught, pour it into a goblet of litmus whose color has been changed to red by an acid, and notice that the blue color of the litmus is restored. (If too much acid has been added to the litmus it will be difficult to make it blue again.)

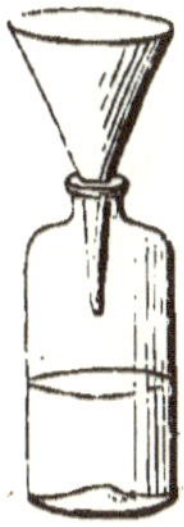

We see in these experiments that some substances have the power to bring back the blue color of litmus after it has been turned red by acids. Now, the most common substances of this kind are called *alkalies*. Ammonia is an alkali, so are potash and soda.

Fig. 25.

Acid or Alkali? Ex. 158.—Having a bottle and a cork which fits its neck, take a wire and run one end of it through the cork, so that when the cork is put into the neck of the bottle the wire will hang down some distance inside. Now take the cork in the hand and hold the other end of the wire in the fire until it is very hot. Plunge this hot wire into a vessel of sulphur. By this means considerable sulphur will cling to the wire. Now again hold the end of the wire in fire to inflame the sulphur upon it, and then plunge the burning sulphur into the bottle. It will continue to burn for a little while, filling the bottle with white fumes. These white fumes are quite different from either the sulphur or the air: a new compound has been formed by the burning sulphur.

Remove the cork and wire and pour a little blue-litmus water into the bottle. Shake it well, putting the hand over the mouth of the bottle to keep the contents from escaping, and *notice* the change of color. Is the new compound an acid or an alkali?

The name of this new substance is *sulphurous acid*. The same white fumes are made when a match is lighted.

Ex. 159.—Put some water into a goblet, and mix with it just enough blue litmus to give it a distinctly blue color. Then take a glass tube: put one end into the colored water, the other into the mouth, and breathe the air from the lungs out through it in bubbles through the water. After a little while notice the change in the color of the water: it turns to red.

This experiment shows that an acid is contained in the breath as it comes from the lungs: it is called *carbonic acid*.

Nitrogen and Oxygen. Ex. 160.—Prepare a bottle, with cork and wire, just as was done in Ex. 158 ; the bottle may be in this case a large one. Cover the end of the wire with sulphur, and let it burn in the bottle, as in the other experiment. Have a second cork fitting the bottle: take the cork and wire out, putting the other cork quickly in. Cover the wire a second time with sulphur, and burn it in the bottle. Repeat this until the sulphur quite refuses to burn in the bottle. Then turn the bottle cork downward: plunge its neck into a basin of water: take the cork out, being careful to let no air get in, and leave the bottle thus inverted in the water. After some considerable time, notice that the white fumes in the bottle are not as dense as they were. We see that the water is taking them out. Finally, they will all disappear. Notice then that the water has risen in the bottle a ways, and that the air (as it seems to be) above the water is again clear.* Now *cork the bottle* again, and *afterward* remove it from the water and stand it upon the table.

---

* If the teacher will perform this part of the experiment beforehand. he need not wait for the water to take the fumes out. He can tell the pupils

Next take a bit of candle; fasten it to the lower end of a wire (which may be bent upward for the purpose) (Fig. 26), and having lighted it, take the cork from the bottle and plunge the candle in. The flame is extinguished as if it had been plunged into water. If it were air in the bottle the candle would continue to burn, so that what seems to be air in the bottle is not.

Now, this gas is what is called *nitrogen*.

From this experiment several things may be learned:

First.—The sulphur, burned in air, *left* only nitrogen: then *nitrogen is a constituent of air.*

Fig. 26.

Second.—We look at the bottle and see that nitrogen is a *gas, colorless,* and *transparent* as air itself.

Third.—Nitrogen *extinguishes flame* as quickly as water would.

Fourth.—The burning sulphur took *something out of the air* of the bottle to leave the nitrogen. This *something* combined with the sulphur to form the new compound—the white fumes.

Now this substance taken out of the air by the burning sulphur is what is called *Oxygen.* So that we learn:

Fifth.—That oxygen is another constituent of the air.

The sulphur took the oxygen out of the air while burning; now, it is a fact that when *any* substance burns in air the oxygen of the air is being used up. If it were not for the oxygen in the air there would be no such thing as fire known upon the earth.

Ex. 161.—Now light the candle and again plunge it

that he did the same thing with the other bottle, and that now, after standing so long, the fumes are all gone, and then go on with the work. Always let the bottle which they have been using, stand, that they may see the air clear in it also afterward.

into the bottle which held the nitrogen (Ex. 160), and
which has been left, *standing open*, on the table. Notice
that the flame is *not* quickly extinguished, as it was before.
The nitrogen has left the bottle, we see: it must have
gone up out of the open bottle into the air of the room.

This experiment teaches us that nitrogen is *lighter than
air*.

Hydrogen. Ex. 162.—Put some clippings of zinc
(sheets of zinc are used under stoves) into a wide-mouth
bottle.   Let the bottom of the bottle be more than
covered with them, and then pour water in to more than
cover the zinc.   Next pour a little sulphuric acid into the
bottle.   In a few moments the liquid will begin to foam :
if not, then add a little more acid, for the "boiling"
should be violent enough to make the foaming fill the
bottle half full.   After this violent chemical action has
gone on for a few minutes, and while still violent, bring a
lighted match to the mouth of the bottle.   An explosion
will be heard, and a flame will at the same time appear
at the mouth of the bottle—sometimes running down
into it.

We see that a gas is produced in this experiment which
is combustible. This combustible gas is called *Hydrogen*.

Ex. 163.—Wrap a towel around a bottle containing
zinc and water, as in the last experiment.   Pour in the
acid as before, but touch the match to the mouth of the
bottle *very soon* after the action begins.   The explosion
may be more noticeable in this experiment.

The object of the cloth is to prevent the glass from
flying and causing injury if, as *very rarely* occurs, the
explosion should be strong enough to break the bottle.
Another proper caution is to tie the match to the end of

a wire or stick, so that the hand would be at a distance when the explosion occurs.

Now notice that in this experiment the hydrogen has not had time to drive the air all out of the bottle, so that there is a *mixture* of air and the gas when the explosion occurs.

We see that hydrogen and air form an explosive mixture.

On this account great care should be taken, in all experiments with hydrogen, to *expel all air from the apparatus* before using the gas.

Ex. 164.—Prepare a cork for the bottle in which hydrogen is to be made, by making a hole through the middle of it and inserting the end of the stem of a tobacco-pipe, so that when the cork is put into the neck of the bottle it shall fit *air-tight*—the pipe-stem reaching above it. The zinc and water being put into the bottle, add enough sulphuric acid, and then quickly insert the cork. Wait until you are sure that the air has been driven out by the hydrogen, and then bring a lighted match to the upper end of the pipe-stem. The hydrogen takes fire as it issues, and burns with a steady flame (Fig. 27).

Notice the flame, and you will see that it gives a feeble light, but:

Ex. 165.—Insert a small wire in the flame and you will find it quickly glowing with a red heat.

Fig. 27.

The flame of burning hydrogen is the source of little light, but of very intense heat.

Carbonic Acid. Ex. 166.—Cover the bottom of a glass jar (it may be a common fruit-can) with "baking soda," and pour upon it—a little at a time—some strong vinegar. Watch the violent boiling, or, as it is properly called, effervescence, which occurs. Take a bit of candle; fasten it to the lower end of a wire, which is bent upward to support it. Light the candle and pass it down into the jar: the flame will be put out as it enters the gas given off by this chemical action.

Notice also that the gas in the jar is colorless and transparent. Is it nitrogen? We will see in another experiment.

Ex. 167.—Let the jar containing the gas stand for some time *open* upon the table after the effervescence has stopped. Insert the lighted candle again: it is seen to be again extinguished,—showing that this gas is heavier than air, and hence is not nitrogen.

This colorless gas, which extinguishes flame and is heavier than air, is called *Carbonic acid.*

Ex. 168.—Take a piece of candle, an inch in length, and fasten it upon a cork. This may be done by dropping some melted tallow upon the middle of the cork and pressing the lower end of the candle down upon it, until it hardens. Light the candle, and put it into a jar, or very wide-mouthed bottle. Cover the jar with a plate. The candle standing upon the bottom of the jar goes on burning for a little while, but begins to grow dim, and finally expires. Take the plate from the jar. A stiff wire which has been sharpened with a file may now be stuck down into the cork, and by this means the candle may be lifted out. Next pour a little *lime-water* * into the jar, and notice that on shaking it about it becomes milky. What

---

* Lime-water may be prepared by taking a little slacked lime, putting it into a bottle, filling the bottle with water, and then shaking it thoroughly. Let the lime afterward settle, and then pour off the clear water above into another vessel for use.

makes this change? Air will not do it, Nitrogen would not stay in the open jar, so that it cannot be nitrogen; much less can it be hydrogen. The gas which was in the jar, to turn the lime-water milky, was colorless; it put out the flame of the candle, and it was heavier than air. It seems to have been carbonic acid gas. As a matter of fact, this gas is the only one which will turn lime-water milky.

But what produced this gas in the jar? It must have been the burning candle.

All common flames like this one produces carbonic acid gas.

Ex. 169.—Put a little lime-water into a goblet, and, taking a glass tube, or even a *straw*, put one end into the water, the other into the mouth, and breathe the breath out through the liquid. After a breath or two, the lime-water will be seen to be milky, thus showing the presence of carbonic acid gas.

We learn from this experiment that carbonic acid is one of the things given off from the lungs in breathing.

Ex. 170.—Breathe into a clean and dry glass jar: its sides are instantly covered with dew. Showing that water-vapor is another thing given off from the lungs in breathing.

Carbonic acid and water are constantly being produced in the process of breathing. The first of these is made up of carbon and oxygen: the second of hydrogen and oxygen. The oxygen for both is furnished by the air taken into the lungs: the carbon and the hydrogen are furnished by waste particles or impurities of the system. The oxygen from the lungs enters the blood-vessels, and goes throughout all parts of the circulation, meeting these waste particles in its course. It decomposes them: com-

bines with their carbon and hydrogen, and then, as carbonic acid and water, goes back to the lungs, from which
these substances are thrown out into the air. In this way
the blood is purified.

Flame. Ex. 171.—Spread the wick of an alcohol
lamp, so that, lighting it, a large flame may be obtained.
Plunge the sulphur end of a match into the dark center
of this flame, and notice that while the wood burns in the
edge of the flame, the more combustible *end of the match
does not burn* in the center of it.

Ex. 172.—Take a long splinter or rod of pine wood,
freshly smoothed, that its surface may be white, and lay
it horizontally across the alcohol flame, just above the
wick. When the stick begins to burn remove it, and
notice that it is scorched in *two places*. The part which
was over the center of the flame is unharmed.

Ex. 173.—Press a piece of white paper, held *horizontally*, quickly down into the flame of the alcohol lamp, to
a place just above the wick. As soon as the scorching
begins to be seen through the paper take it quickly away.
The paper will be burned in the shape of a ring. That
part which was directly over the wick is unburned.

Ex. 174.—The following experiment may be added to
this list, provided great care is taken to follow directions:
otherwise accident might happen.

A common dinner-plate, when inverted, gives us a very
shallow dish, the bottom of a plate being, as you will see,
surrounded with a slightly elevated rim. Put a plate upon
the table, bottom upward, and pour alcohol into the shallow dish thus obtained, being very careful that none of the
fluid runs over upon the table or even upon the sides of
the plate. Take a cork, about an inch in diameter: put a

little gunpowder upon top of it, and stand it right in the center of the alcohol on the plate. Take a lighted match and touch the alcohol at *one edge of the plate ;* it will take fire : the flame will instantly spread all over the top of the plate, and, if no breeze waft it against the cork, the gunpowder will remain some time, *in the center of the flame*, unharmed !

These experiments clearly teach us that the interior of the alcohol flame is not in a state of combustion. The same experiments, except the last one, may be made with a candle-flame with much the same results. The interior of all ordinary flames are, like that of the alcohol-lamp, not burning. This central part of a flame consists of combustible gas, and is surrounded by the burning envelope.

Ex. 175.—Repeat Experiment 164 with apparatus shown in Fig. 27. Having thus obtained a hydrogen-flame, remember that it is being produced by the hydrogen from the bottle and the oxygen in the air. Now, hold over this flame a clean and thoroughly dry glass jar. Its sides will be seen to become instantly covered with dew.

Now, this water is the result of the action between hydrogen and oxygen in the flame, and hence the experiment teaches that water is made up of the two substances, hydrogen and oxygen.

Ex. 176.—Now hold a clean and dry jar in the same way over the flame of the alcohol-lamp : its sides are soon dimmed with dew also. Let the same thing be done with a candle and with other flames. Water will be, in every case, deposited upon the sides of the jar.

But, since water consists of hydrogen and oxygen. these results show that these two substances take part in the production of the flames. Water is a product of all ordinary combustion in flames : the oxygen is furnished from the air : the hydrogen from the body burning.

Ex. 177.—Press the bottom of a cold dinner-plate down upon the flame of a candle. A moment afterward take the plate from the flame, and notice the black soot which is collected where the flame burned against it. There is something beside hydrogen and oxygen, we see, taking part in the production of this flame. The black soot is *carbon*. The flame of a burning stick, and indeed almost any common flame, will furnish carbon upon a solid body held in it. And yet no carbon is seen when a flame burns freely. Why ?

Ex. 178.—Fix a bit of candle upon a cork, by dropping a little of the melted wax or tallow upon its top and pressing the bottom of the candle upon it until cold. Light the candle and stand it on the table, and bring an inverted glass jar down over it. The candle will burn freely for a little while, but at length it will burn more dimly, and finally go out. Turn the glass-jar right side up and pour into it a little *lime-water*. After shaking it about a little, the lime-water will become whitish, showing the presence of *carbonic acid*.

Now, carbonic acid consists of oxygen and carbon, and it has been formed in the flame. Its oxygen has been furnished by the air, but its carbon must have come from the candle. And now we see what becomes of the carbon when a flames burns freely. It combines with oxygen of the air, and forms carbonic acid gas, which, being invisible, passes unseen off into the air.

We see from these experiments that water and carbonic gas are produced by the combustion in ordinary flames. The hydrogen and the carbon for these are furnished by the fuel which burns, while the oxygen comes from the air. Combustion in all common instances is nothing but a chemical action between the oxygen of the air and the elements of the fuel.

Laboratory Physics

Hammel's Observation Blanks in Physics

By WILLIAM C. A. HAMMEL, Professor of Physics in Maryland State School. Boards, Quarto, 42 pages. Illustrated. . . . . . . 30 cents

These Observation Blanks are designed for use as a Pupil's Laboratory Manual and Note Book for the first term's work in the study of Physics. They combine in convenient form descriptions and illustrations of the apparatus required for making experiments in Physics, with special reference to the elements of Air, Liquids, and Heat; directions for making the required apparatus from simple inexpensive materials, and for performing the experiments, etc. The book is supplied with blanks for making drawings of the apparatus and for the pupil to record what he has observed and inferred concerning the experiment and the principle illustrated.

The experiments are carefully selected in the light of experience and arranged in logical order. The treatment throughout is in accordance with the best laboratory practice of the day.

Hon. W. T. Harris, U. S. Commissioner of Education, says of these Blanks:

"I have seen several attempts to assist the work of pupils engaged in the study of Physics, but I have never seen anything which promises to be of such practical assistance as Hammel's Observation Blanks."

Physics

Appletons' School Physics

By JOHN D. QUACKENBOS, A.M., M.D., ALFRED M. MAYER, Ph.D., SILAS W. HOLMAN, S.B., FRANCIS E. NIPHER, A.M., and FRANCIS B. CROCKER, E.M.

Cloth, 12mo, 552 pages $1.20

This book is a thoroughly modern text-book on Natural Philosophy, which reflects the most advanced pedagogical methods and the latest laboratory practice. It is adapted for use in the higher grades of grammar schools, and for high schools and academies.

Cooley's New Text-Book of Physics

By LE ROY C. COOLEY, Ph.D. Cloth, 12mo, 327 pages 90 cents

An elementary course in Natural Philosophy for high schools and academies. It is brief, modern, logical in arrangement, and thoroughly systematic.

Steele's Popular Physics

By J. DORMAN STEELE, Ph.D. Cloth, 12mo, 392 pages $1.00

This new work is a thorough revision of the popular text-book, " Fourteen Weeks in Physics," so long and favorably known. It presents a thoroughly scientific treatment of the principles of the science in such an attractive style and manner as to awaken and hold the interest of pupils from the first.

Stewart's Physics—SCIENCE PRIMER SERIES

By BALFOUR STEWART. Flexible cloth, 18mo, 168 pages 35 cents

This little book contains an exposition of the fundamental principles of Physics, suited to pupils in elementary grades or for the general reader.

Trowbridge's New Physics

By JOHN TROWBRIDGE, S.D. Cloth, 12mo, 387 pages . $1.20

A thoroughly modern work, intended as a class manual of Physics for colleges and advanced preparatory schools.

Hammel's Observation Blanks in Physics

By WILLIAM C. A. HAMMEL.

Flexible, quarto, 42 pages. Illustrated . . . . 30 cents

A pupil's laboratory manual and note-book for the first term's work. Each pupil to make his own apparatus and then to perform the experiments as outlined. Blanks are left in which the pupil writes his observations and the principles illustrated. It is simple, practical, and inexpensive.

Copies of any of the above books will be sent prepaid to any address, on receipt of the price, by the Publishers :

American Book Company

New York • Cincinnati • Chicago
(90)

Zoölogy and Natural History

Burnet's School Zoölogy
By MARGARETTA BURNET.   Cloth, 12mo, 216 pages   .   **75 cents**
A new text-book for high schools and academies, by a practical teacher; sufficiently elementary for beginners and full enough for the usual course in Natural History.

Needham's Elementary Lessons in Zoölogy
By JAMES G. NEEDHAM, M.S.   Cloth, 12mo, 302 pages   .   **90 cents**
An elementary text-book for high schools, academies, normal schools and preparatory college classes.   Special attention is given to the study by scientific methods, laboratory practice, microscopic study and practical zoötomy.

Cooper's Animal Life
By SARAH COOPER.   Cloth, 12mo, 427 pages   .   .   .   **$1.25**
An attractive book for young people.   Admirably adapted for supplementary readings in Natural History.

Holders' Elementary Zoölogy
By C. F. HOLDER, and J. B. HOLDER, M.D.
Cloth, 12mo, 401 pages **$1.20**
A text-book for high school classes and other schools of secondary grade.

Hooker's Natural History
By WORTHINGTON HOOKER, M.D.   Cloth, 12mo, 394 pages   **90 cents**
Designed either for the use of schools or for the general reader.

Morse's First Book in Zoölogy
By EDWARD S. MORSE, Ph.D.   Boards, 12mo, 204 pages   **87 cents**
For the first study of animal life.   The examples presented are such as are common and familiar.

Nicholson's Text-Book of Zoölogy
By H. A. NICHOLSON, M.D.   Cloth, 12mo, 421 pages   .   **$1.38**
Revised edition.   Adapted for advanced grades of high schools or academies and for first work in college classes.

Steele's Popular Zoölogy
By J. DORMAN STEELE, Ph.D., and J. W. P. JENKS.
Cloth, 12mo, 369 pages **$1.20**
For academies, preparatory schools and general reading.   This popular work is marked by the same clearness of method and simplicity of statement that characterize all Prof. Steele's text-books in the Natural Sciences.

Tenneys' Natural History of Animals
By SANBORN TENNEY and ABBEY A. TENNEY.
Revised Edition.   Cloth, 12mo, 281 pages   .   .   .   **$1.20**
This new edition has been entirely reset and thoroughly revised, the recent changes in classification introduced, and the book in all respects brought up to date.

Treat's Home Studies in Nature
By Mrs. MARY TREAT.   Cloth, 12mo, 244 pages   .   .   **90 cents**
An interesting and instructive addition to the works on Natural History.

Copies of any of the above books will be sent prepaid to any address, on receipt of the price, by the Publishers :

American Book Company

New York   •   Cincinnati   •   Chicago

Geology

Dana's Geological Story Briefly Told

By JAMES D. DANA. Cloth, 12mo, 302 pages .   .   . $1.15

A new edition of this popular work for beginners in the study and for the general reader. The book has been entirely rewritten, and improved by the addition of many new illustrations and interesting descriptions of the latest phases and discoveries of the science. In contents and dress it is an attractive volume either for the reader or student.

Dana's New Text-Book of Geology

By JAMES D. DANA. Cloth, 12mo, 422 pages .   .   . $2.00

A text-book for classes in secondary schools and colleges. This standard work has been thoroughly revised and considerably enlarged and freshly illustrated to represent the latest demands of the science.

Dana's Manual of Geology

By JAMES D. DANA.

Cloth, 8vo, 1087 pages. 1575 Illustrations $5 00

Fourth revised edition. This great work was thoroughly revised and entirely rewritten under the direct supervision of its author, just before his death. It is recognized as a standard authority in the science both in Europe and America, and is used as a manual of instruction in all the higher institutions of learning.

Le Conte's Compend of Geology

By JOSEPH LE CONTE, LL.D. Cloth, 12mo, 399 pages . $1.20

Designed for high schools, academies and all secondary schools.

Steele's Fourteen Weeks in Geology

By J. DORMAN STEELE, Ph.D. Cloth, 12mo, 280 pages . $1.00

A popular book for elementary classes and the general reader.

Andrews's Elementary Geology

By E. B. ANDREWS, LL.D. Cloth, 12mo, 283 pages . $1 00

Adapted for elementary classes. Contains a special treatment of the geology of the Mississippi Valley.

Nicholson's Text-Book of Geology

By H. A. NICHOLSON, M.D. Cloth, 12mo, 520 pages . $1.05

A brief course for higher classes and adapted for general reading.

Williams's Applied Geology

By S. G. WILLIAMS, Ph.D. Cloth, 12mo, 386 pages .   . $1.20

A treatise on the industrial relations of geological structure; and on the nature, occurrence, and uses of substances derived from geological sources.

Copies of any of the above books will be sent prepaid to any address, on receipt of the price, by the Publishers :

American Book Company

New York   •   Cincinnati   •   Chicago

Text-Books in Astronomy

Bowen's Astronomy by Observation

By ELIZA A. BOWEN.

Boards, quarto, 94 pages.   Colored Maps and Illustrations $1.00

An elementary text-book for schools, and especially adapted for use as an atlas to accompany any other text-book in astronomy.   Careful directions are given when, how and where to find the heavenly bodies, and the quarto pages admit star maps and views on a large scale.

Gillet and Rolfe's Astronomies

By J. A. GILLET and W. J. ROLFE.

First Book in Astronomy.   Short Course.   220 pages .   . $1.00
Astronomy.   415 pages 1.40

These books have been prepared by practical teachers and contain nothing beyond the comprehension of pupils in secondary schools.

Lockyer's Astronomies

By J. N. LOCKYER, F.R.S.

Astronomy.   (Science Primer Series.)   136 pages   .   35 cents
Elementary Lessons in Astronomy.   312 pages .   .   . $1.2?

The aim throughout these books is to give a connected view of the whole subject rather than to discuss any particular parts of it, and to supply facts and ideas founded thereon, to serve as a basis for subsequent study.

Ray's New Elements of Astronomy

By SELIM H. PEABODY, Ph.D., LL.D.

Cloth, 12mo, 352 pages $1 20

The elements of astronomy, with numerous engravings and star maps. In the revised edition, the scope and method of the original is retained, with the addition of all the results of established discovery.   The book treats of the facts, principles, and processes of the science, presuming only that the pupil is acquainted with the simplest principles of mechanics and physics.

Steele's New Descriptive Astronomy

By J. DORMAN STEELE, Ph.D.   Cloth, 12mo, 338 pages . $1.00

This book is written in the same interesting and popular manner as other books of the Steele Series, and is intended for the inspiration of youth rather than for the information of scientific scholars.   The book conforms to the latest discoveries and approved theories of the science. It supplies an adequate course in astronomy for all secondary schools and college preparatory classes.

Copies of any of the above books will be sent prepaid to any address, on receipt of the price, by the Publishers:

American Book Company

New York   •   Cincinnati   •   Chicago

Physiology and Hygiene

Kellogg's First Book in Physiology and Hygiene
  Cloth, 12mo, 174 pages . . . . 40 cents
Kellogg's Second Book in Physiology and Hygiene
  Cloth, 12mo, 291 pages . . . . 80 cents
  These two books constitute an entirely new and well graded series for the study of Physiology and Hygiene in schools. The subjects are treated in a natural and logical order and arranged in a form suitable for class instruction. The important subjects of sanitation and temperance are thoroughly treated from a scientific and physiological standpoint.

Smith's Primer of Physiology and Hygiene
  Cloth, 12mo, 174 pages . . . . 30 cents
Smith's Elementary Physiology and Hygiene
  Cloth, 12mo, 225 pages . . . . 50 cents
  A complete and symmetrical series in which the important facts of Physiology and Hygiene are presented in an interesting manner. The Primer is designed for beginners in the study and the second book for classes in the intermediate grades.

Steele's Hygienic Physiology
  Cloth, 12mo, 400 pages $1.00
  This standard text-book has been thoroughly revised and considerably enlarged. It contains all the excellent and popular features that have given Dr. Steele's Science Series such wide use in schools throughout the country.
  THE SAME, abridged. Cloth, 12mo, 192 pages . . 50 cents

Tracy's Essentials of Anatomy, Physiology and Hygiene
  Cloth, 12mo, 345 pages $1.00
  A practical, thorough and scientific text-book of an advanced grade for the use of classes in High Schools, Academies, Normal Schools, and for private students.

Johonnot and Bouton's How We Live
  Cloth, 12mo, 178 pages . . . . 40 cents
  An elementary text-book for beginners in which special attention is given to the laws of Hygiene.

Walker's Health Lessons
  Cloth, 12mo, 194 pages . . . . 48 cents
  A book for beginners, presenting the subjects in an interesting and readable form suitable for supplementary readings.

Copies of any of the above books will be sent prepaid to any address, on receipt of the price, by the Publishers:

American Book Company

New York   •   Cincinnati   •   Chicago

Physical Geography

Appletons' Physical Geography

By JOHN D. QUACKENBOS, JOHN S. NEWBERRY, CHARLES H. HITCHCOCK, W. LE CONTE STEVENS, WM. H. DALL, HENRY GANNETT, C. HART MERRIAM, NATHANIEL L. BRITTON, GEORGE F. KUNZ and Lieut. GEO. M. STONEY.

Cloth, quarto, 140 pages $1.60

Prepared on a new and original plan. Richly illustrated with engravings, diagrams and maps in color, and including a separate chapter on the geological history and the physical features of the United States. The aim has been to popularize the study of Physical Geography by furnishing a complete, attractive, carefully condensed text-book.

Cornell's Physical Geography

Boards, quarto, 104 pages $1.12

Revised edition, with such alterations and additions as were found necessary to bring the work in all respects up to date.

Hinman's Eclectic Physical Geography

Cloth, 12mo, 382 pages $1.00

By RUSSELL HINMAN. A model text-book of the subject in a new and convenient form. It embodies a strictly scientific and accurate treatment of Physiography and other branches of Physical Geography. Adapted for classes in high schools, academies and colleges, and for private students. The text is fully illustrated by numerous maps, charts, cuts and diagrams.

Guyot's Physical Geography

Cloth, quarto, 124 pages $1.60

By ARNOLD GUYOT. Thoroughly revised and supplied with newly engraved maps, illustrations, etc. A standard work by one of the ablest of modern geographers. All parts of the subject are presented in their true relations and in their proper subordination.

Monteith's New Physical Geography

Cloth, quarto, 144 pages $1.00

An elementary work adapted for use in common and grammar schools, as well as in high schools.

Copies of any of the above books will be sent prepaid to any address, on receipt of the price, by the Publishers:

American Book Company

New York • Cincinnati ♦ Chicago

Standard Text-Books in Botany

Gray's How Plants Grow. (Introductory Book)	80 cents
Gray's How Plants Behave	54 cents
For Beginners in Primary and Intermediate Schools.	
Gray's Lessons in Botany. (Revised)	94 cents
Gray's Field, Forest and Garden Botany. (Flora) . . .	$1.44
Gray's School and Field Botany. (The Standard Text-Book)	$1.80
For Students in High Schools, Academies and Seminaries.	
Gray's Manual of Botany. (Flora)	$1.62
Gray's Lessons and Manual. (In one volume) . . .	$2.16
For Advanced Students, Teachers, and Practical Botanists.	
Coulter's Botany of the Rocky Mountains	$1.62
A flora adapted to the mountain section of the United States.	
Gray and Coulter's Text-Book of Western Botany . . .	$2.16
Being Gray's Lessons and Coulter's Manual bound in one volume.	
Gray's Structural Botany	$2.00
Goodale's Physiological Botany	$2.00
Dana's Plants and their Children	65 cents
Herrick's Chapters on Plant Life	60 cents
Hooker's Botany. (Science Primer Series)	35 cents
Hooker's Child's Book of Nature. PART I. PLANTS .	44 cents
Steele's Fourteen Weeks in Botany	$1.00
Wood's How to Study Plants	$1.00
Same as above work, with added chapters on Physiological and Systematic Botany.	
Wood's Lessons in Botany. (Revised)	90 cents
Wood's New American Botanist and Florist. (Revised) .	$1.75
Wood's Descriptive Botany	$1.25
Being the flora of the American Botanist and Florist.	
Wood's Class Book of Botany	$2.50
A standard work for Advanced Classes and for the Student's Library.	
Youmans's First Book in Botany	64 cents
Youmans's Descriptive Botany	$1.20
Bentley's Physiological Botany	$1.20
A sequel to Youmans's Descriptive Botany.	
Willis's Practical Flora	$1.50
A valuable supplementary aid to any text-book in the study of Botany.	

Copies of the above books will be sent, prepaid, to any address on receipt of the price by the Publishers:

American Book Company

New York   •   Cincinnati   •   Chicago

Concrete Geometry for Beginners

By A. R. HORNBROOK, A.M.

Teacher of Mathematics in High School, Evansville, Ind.

Linen, 12mo, 201 pages. Price, 75 cents

This little work has been prepared by a practical teacher of mathematics as an elementary text-book for beginners in the study. In scope, plan and grade, it is adapted to follow the course in mathematics usually pursued in Common and Grammar Schools, or to precede the study of Demonstrative Geometry in the High School.

Some of the distinctive methods illustrated and applied in the book are the following:

Experimental Work. The work is eminently practical, its material and methods being the results of actual experimental work in private and public schools in discovering the effects produced upon the minds of pupils by mathematical instruction, and in seeking to adjust such instruction to the mental capacity of the pupils, so that it may be most readily assimilated and understood by them.

Rational Development. This little book, without giving rules to be learned or formal modes of reasoning to be copied, leads the child to construct, to observe, to compute, to infer for himself and to report the result of his operations in mathematical language.

Progressive Plan. The plan of the book is to follow the method of gradually developing each subject by questions, giving necessary information and directions in notes, thus allowing full scope to the skilful teacher who can expand the subjects and adjust the material to the special needs of each class.

Laboratory Methods. The use of this convenient text-book for a few weeks before taking up Demonstrative Geometry, will give a class that familiarity with geometric forms and facts which is essential to logical reasoning, and will thus greatly increase the chances of rapid and successful work. The great number of problems and their very gradual increase in difficulty, admirably adapt the work for use by the Laboratory Method.

Copies of this book will be sent prepaid to any address, on receipt of the price, by the Publishers :

American Book Company

New York   -   Cincinnati   -   Chicago

Elementary Algebra

Milne's Elements of Algebra

Cloth, 12mo, 200 pages   .   .   .   **60 cents**

This is a beginner's book intended for classes commencing the study of Algebra in Common Schools, Grammar Schools or High Schools. It presents the elementary facts of the science in such a simple manner that the pupil's interest will be awakened, and the steps are so gradual that his progress will be easy and encouraging. Abundant examples insure a thorough understanding of each principle presented, and the solutions required are clear and illustrative. The use of the book in classes will lay a sound foundation for more advanced work in the study.

Sabin and Lowry's Elementary Lessons in Algebra

Cloth, 12mo, 128 pages   .   .   **50 cents**

This work is designed to meet the demand for a distinctly elementary Algebra suitable for the higher Grammar School grades. It consists of a series of elementary lessons, inculcating a thorough knowledge of algebraic processes and giving facility in the use of algebraic symbols. The work makes an easy transition from arithmetic to algebraic processes, and the treatment throughout is simple and logical. The examples for practice are numerous and well graded.

Copies of the above books, or any of our Higher Algebras (see list), will be sent prepaid to any address, on receipt of the price, by the Publishers :

American Book Company

New York   •   Cincinnati   •   Chicago

(85)

Burnet's Zoölogy

FOR

HIGH SCHOOLS AND ACADEMIES

BY

MARGARETTA BURNET

Teacher of Zoölogy, Woodward High School, Cincinnati, O.

Cloth, 12mo, 216 pages. Illustrated. Price, 75 cents

This new text-book on Zoölogy is intended for classes in High Schools, Academies, and other Secondary Schools. While sufficiently elementary for beginners in the study it is full and comprehensive enough for students pursuing a regular course in the Natural Sciences. It has been prepared by a practical teacher, and is the direct result of school-room experience, field observation and laboratory practice.

The design of the book is to give a good general knowledge of the subject of Zoölogy, to cultivate an interest in nature study, and to encourage the pupil to observe and to compare for himself and then to arrange and classify his knowledge. Only typical or principal forms are described, and in their description only such technical terms are used as are necessary, and these are carefully defined.

Each subject is fully illustrated, the illustrations being selected and arranged to aid the pupil in understanding the structure of each form.

Copies of Burnet's School Zoölogy will be sent prepaid to any address, on receipt of the price, by the Publishers:

American Book Company

New York • Cincinnati • Chicago